Bats or Swallows

Bats or Swallows

BY TERI VLASSOPOULOS

Invisible Publishing

Halifax & Toronto

Library and Archives Canada Cataloguing in Publication

Vlassopoulos, Teri, 1979-
        Bats or swallows / Teri Vlassopoulos.

ISBN 978-1-926743-07-3

        I. Title.

PS8643.L38B38 2010   C813'.6   C2010-905210-2

Cover & Interior designed by Megan Fildes

Typeset in Laurentian and Slate by Megan Fildes
With thanks to type designer Rod McDonald

Printed and bound in Canada

Invisible Publishing
Halifax & Toronto
www.invisiblepublishing.com

We acknowledge the support of the Canada Council for the Arts which last
year invested $20.1 million in writing and publishing throughout Canada.

Invisible Publishing recognizes the support of the Province of Nova Scotia
through the Department of Tourism, Culture & Heritage. We are pleased
to work in partnership with the Culture Division to develop and promote
our cultural resources for all Nova Scotians.

 Canada Council   Conseil des Arts
for the Arts   du Canada

A SECRET HANDSHAKE

THE SUMMER I WAS TWELVE YEARS OLD and my brother Mitch was fourteen, we had a secret handshake. It was subtle. Often when people invent secret handshakes, they are complex, acrobatic things involving thrusts, fists, snapping. Ours was quiet. The secret part: when you shake hands, you do this thing with your right foot, pivot it a little. Because, we decided, what was the point of a secret handshake when anyone could see what you were doing, when someone could be watching with a spycam hidden in their lapel, studying your hands or anticipating pressure points? No one looks at the feet. We took our handshake seriously and that summer we discussed it while we sat by the pool in the backyard. How could we introduce it to a real secret society? Should we just start one ourselves? And if we started a secret society, who would be allowed in?

Mom sometimes hovered in the background of these

conversations, adjusting the sprinkler, fishing stray leaves out of the pool, wiping down patio furniture. One evening after listening to us she said, "You know, Ray was a Freemason." She said it all breezy and casual, and we watched her pick up the sprinkler, move it to a dry patch and walk back to the house without getting wet.

When my mother was nineteen she married her high school sweetheart. Ray was twenty-one and from the pictures I've seen, gorgeous. I know that everyone looks good when they're in their early twenties and in love—there's that *glow*—but Ray was honest-to-god movie star good-looking. I mean, he was cool. And then Mitch was born. Mitchum. Ray wanted a name that was trustworthy and respectable, but had a tinge of Hollywood to it. There are pictures of the three of them, my mother and Ray grinning down at baby Mitch. They looked happy.

Three months after those photos were taken, while Mitchum was asleep in a laundry basket, drooling over their white shag rug, Ray was killed in a car accident. It was an icy night and another car lost control and hit him from behind. Barely one year later, Mom remarried. Her second husband, my father, was someone she'd also known in high school. I was born soon after that.

I grew up with this story, accepted it without question, and it wasn't until that summer, the summer of our secret handshake, that it occurred to me how strange it was: within two years my mother had married and had a baby, lost her husband and remarried.

After Mom told us about Ray's direct involvement with a real secret society, Mitch and I were silent for a good minute.

"Ray was a Freemason?" I asked. Screamed it, maybe.

"Weird." Mitch's response was less enthusiastic and shrieky than mine. He didn't say anything else and so, embarrassed, I got up from where we were sitting. I walked through the newly positioned sprinkler to get damp and then I jumped into the pool. Mitch didn't join me. He didn't say much for the rest of the evening, but I could guess what he was thinking.

Mitch was still just young enough that he could tolerate and even enjoy random research projects with me. Freemasonry was one of the secret societies we studied at the library. We had found a book about it and memorized a few facts. It was the kind of society whose rituals were passed along bloodlines. I knew that Mitch was thinking that if Ray hadn't died, he would've passed on its secrets to him. Mitch would've had connections that could carry him through life. He would've stood a better chance of being Prime Minister or a CEO or even the owner of a chain of fast food restaurants, like Dave Thomas, founder of Wendy's, who was also a Mason. Instead Mitch was stuck inventing stupid handshakes with his kid sister.

After my swim I went to see Dad in the kitchen. I stood by the counter and thought about asking him about Ray, but I wasn't sure what I wanted to know. I fidgeted until he told me to help him with dinner. He was making stuffed tomatoes and peppers and was heaping tablespoons of rice and ground meat into their open cavities. I would only eat the stuffing and Mitch preferred the skins, so we would usually trade plates halfway through these meals. It was a good deal. That evening Mitch refused to eat with us. He made a big production of making his own dinner of toast and peanut butter and sitting by the pool alone.

Mom and Dad tried to force him to come to the table, but he ignored them, and they let it go. It was his first silent tantrum. There were more that followed, but at the time it was something new and unexpected. After dinner Mom scraped my discarded tomato and pepper skins into the garbage can and the thwack of the vegetables hitting the bottom of the bin was heavy and wet.

The new information about Ray unleashed something in my brother. I could see him mulling it over, letting it bloom in his bloodstream and knot in his face. Mathematics were introduced into our family: I wasn't Mitch's sister, I was his half-sister. Our nomenclature was also called into question. Mitch grew up calling Dad "Dad," but slowly he started addressing him by his first name. *"Jim."* He tested it out tentatively, but then gained confidence and I would hear him say his name with gusto, incorporating a perfectly timed eye roll. But at the same time, when he mentioned Ray, he still called him "Ray," not "my father," and thankfully not "Dad." I braced myself for that moment.

Rather than discuss the issue, Mitch withdrew into himself and, to my surprise, Mom and Dad let it slide. For a few weeks the house was simply tense, on the cusp. Mitch, as if to further emphasize that something inside of him had changed, stole some of Mom's menthol cigarettes and smoked them in the backyard when Mom and Dad were at work. He didn't hide it from me and from my bedroom window I saw him take drags of those long, skinny cigarettes while he looked up at the sky. My own lungs contracted as I thought of all those times we had begged my mother to stop smoking. Mitch had even once broken the toilet in an attempt to flush them away. His behaviour confused me, but it also slowly infuriated me since it bled into my summer too, distorted it into a different version of what I had expected.

Ray's parents, Mitch's grandparents, lived in Quebec and although they consistently sent Christmas and birthday cards to Mitch, they rarely called or visited us in Toronto. Mitch asked if he could visit them. He had never been, but now decided that he should be given the chance to know his grandparents.

"You already have grandparents," I said to him. "Two sets. You don't need any more."

"You can visit them as long as they *want* you to visit," Mom said, ignoring me. "It's not polite to invite yourself."

Mitch must have contacted them before Mom's etiquette tip because a train ticket arrived via FedEx the next day. I watched Mitch accept the envelope. He threw his shoulders back and deepened his voice when he spoke to the deliveryman, sloppily signing the clipboard handed to him. He went to his room and shoved his clothes into a duffel bag, even the dirty laundry piled on the floor.

"I guess I'll see you when school starts," he told me. It was only the beginning of August.

"You're going for the rest of the summer?"

"Yup."

I stood at his door. "They're letting you stay that long?" I'd peeked at the ticket on the kitchen table and the return date was in a week, not a month. I didn't believe they would allow Mitch, a stranger despite being their grandson, to move in just like that.

When it came time for him to leave, Mom brought him to the train station and I stayed home with Dad.

"What if Mitch doesn't come back?" I asked.

"Why wouldn't he?"

"He doesn't even know French."

"Don't worry," Dad said. "He'll be back by Sunday."

Four days later Mitch called and told Mom that he wanted to stay. I heard the phone pass from Mom to Dad, between Mitch and Ray's parents, and then they hung up and the taut tranquillity of the past few weeks was broken by the sound of my parents fighting. "Just let him stay," Mom said and eventually my father conceded.

There were only three weeks left of summer. I'd taken a stand against enrolling in day camp for my remaining time off and with Mitch gone, I was alone during the day when I wasn't with my friends. Dad would come home for lunch to keep me company, but mostly I read and the time slipped away slowly. For a few days everything was calm again.

One afternoon I saw Dad's car pull into the driveway. I went back to my book and when I looked up he was driving away.

"The strangest thing happened this afternoon," he said to Mom and me when he came home that evening.

He had returned for lunch and checked the mail first before coming in. He noticed that one piece of mail wasn't mail at all, but a red tube. It looked like a stick of dynamite, the way dynamite looks in Bugs Bunny cartoons. He was convinced that it was actual, real dynamite and that it might detonate and blow his daughter and house to bits. So, he stuffed the rest of the mail back into the box, put the tube in the trunk of the car and drove back to work.

"I don't know what I was thinking," he told us. "It seemed like the safest thing to do, to put it in the car and drive away."

"I was almost blown up?" I asked.

"I can't believe you put it in the car," Mom said. "I would've thrown it in the neighbour's yard."

The red tube was a piece of junk mail. He spread its contents on the counter. There was a fake plastic key and an official-looking letter stating that our family had been selected to win a new car if we called the number printed at the bottom of the page. We were almost winners!

After discovering the tube, my father drove to work, parked the car and called the police, who brought in the bomb squad. They popped open the trunk, carefully removed the tube and discovered that it wasn't a bomb, it wasn't dynamite. It wasn't even close. My father apologized and to my disappointment filed a complaint against the company responsible for it, which must have lowered our chance of actually winning anything.

This was probably embarrassing for my father to go through in front of his coworkers, but he didn't seem sheepish. His gut instinct had been to leave me oblivious while he risked his life to drive the dynamite away from his home and me. What if it really had been a bomb, what if the car had exploded somewhere between the house and his office? He would've been a hero, speeding away to save his daughter.

"Can you believe it?" I said after he left the room. I was proud of him. Mom didn't answer me and I sensed that she didn't share the same level of pride.

"Dad has been under some stress recently."

"Is he okay?"

"He's fine," she said, but I didn't believe her. My pride was replaced with something more worrisome: confusion. I wanted to talk about this with Mitch, get his insight. I hadn't spoken to him since he left for Montreal, but I thought he would be able to illuminate the situation for me, tell it to me straight so that I would understand. The next day while I was home alone, I found Ray's parents' number and called. Mitch answered after two rings. When I heard his voice, I wanted to cry. I missed him.

"What are you doing?" I blurted out. "Are you having fun?"

"I am," he said. "I love it here."

"But none of your friends are around."

"I've made friends."

"You have?"

"Why do you care?"

"I don't," I said. The conversation was going all wrong.

"Then why are you calling?"

"I don't know," I said. We hung up soon afterwards and in the end I didn't tell him about the bomb.

Mitch returned Labour Day weekend. He brought a bag of cheese curds and before he'd even taken off his shoes he gave me a handful to try.

"Listen to the way they squeak," he said. His facial expressions were different. Smug, maybe. He had longer hair. I chewed and swallowed and nothing squeaked, but I didn't tell him.

While Mitch had been away, I had kept up my interest in secret societies and borrowed more books about the Freemasons from the library. The society, as it turned out, wasn't really so secretive. There had been investigative reports over the years, so all of their secret stuff was out in the open: their handshake, their code words, what they did at their lodges.

Freemasons have certain positions they make when they

enter a room. They stand a certain way or maybe make an arm gesture. One of these positions involves arranging their feet into a square corner, their bodies tall and straight representing *the rectitude of their actions*. When I learned this, it made me feel as though our secret handshake, with the foot movement, wasn't so original. When Mitch finished talking about Montreal, I told him about this new development, but it didn't resonate with him the same way it had with me.

"That's cool," he said. Case closed. He was floating in the pool on his back, his eyes shut. I jumped in and joined him.

"There's something else," I said. "I know the handshakes!"

There's a distinctive handshake depending on your level within the society, your degree. First degree Masons put pressure with their right thumb on the knuckle of the other man's first finger. Second degree Masons will do the same shake as the first, but with the pressure on the other man's forefinger. Those in the third degree, the highest degree, will use his right thumb to apply pressure between the knuckles of the other man's middle and third finger.

It was confusing reading about these handshakes, like learning how to knit from a diagram or interpreting wordless toy assembly instructions. I kept forgetting which finger was the forefinger. It had to be practiced with another person.

"Mitch, try it with me." We were bobbing in the water. Mitch held an inner tube.

"You can't do the handshake if you're not a part of the society," he said. "It's not right."

"But maybe if you shake someone's hand the right way and it turns out they're a Freemason, they'll think you're interested and invite you to join."

"I don't think it works like that."

"It does! I read about it. They like people who are interested."

Mitch took a deep breath and jackknifed himself underwater so that all that was left was the black rubber tube. He came up behind me. "Why do you care? Girls aren't even allowed in." He climbed out of the pool. "I need a smoke."

To qualify as a member of the Freemasons you must believe wholly in a Supreme Being. The being can be anyone—God, Mohammed, whatever—as long as he/she/it is deemed legitimately Supreme somewhere in the world. The Masonic umbrella term for this being is "The Great Architect of the Universe." Mitch and I thought it sounded funny, like the name of a ride at Canada's Wonderland. Because the term is so long, Freemasons use the acronym TGAOTU in their printed texts. I figured that as long as I found a GAOTU to believe in, I would be a shoo-in. But, Mitch was right about girls not being allowed. It was the first thing I had learned, even before the GAOTU, and then had promptly, conveniently, forgot.

Mitch sat on the picnic bench, smoking. This time he had his own cigarettes. Dad must have been watching from the kitchen because he ran out and yelled, "What are you doing?" and then slapped him.

We both looked blankly at Dad. And then Mitch swore and the two of them started yelling at each other. Mitch's voice had a low tone to it, something that sounded too adult for his fourteen years. They fought like grown-ups. Dad had left the sliding door open and I saw Moonie, our cat, peeking out. Moonie was an indoor cat and I was constantly scrambling to close doors quickly and keep her inside. No one else cared as much. Mom came out back as well, but she just stood there watching.

I dunked my head underwater, and the commotion was

dulled down, cottony, padded by the sound of my own breath. When I came back up Moonie had leapt into the backyard while Mitch and Dad screamed and Mom stood still, simply watching.

I hauled myself out of the pool to catch Moonie and told myself that I needed a secret thing too, that I deserved one. Not Masonry, not cigarettes.

Okay, I thought. *Fine.* I'm ready.

MY SON, THE MAGICIAN

MY SON, JEREMY, was usually a fireman, police officer or businessman. I liked it most when he was a businessman, the way he looked in the cut of his suit and his dress shoes all shined. He tied his tie carefully and slowly standing in front of the hallway mirror. It reminded me of the way he used to practice tying knots when he was a child in the Boy Scouts, that same look of furrowed determination. As a businessman, he wore aftershave, slicked his hair back and carried a briefcase that he found in the basement. Fred, his father, my ex-husband, left it behind when he moved out.

Jeremy never said it out loud, but I know he preferred being a police officer. I could tell by the way he carried himself. Taller, with an aura of self-confidence. He enjoyed the way people looked at him—a man with real authority—when he walked down the street in his uniform. He was most embarrassed when he had to be a fireman, and wouldn't change into the uniform until the last minute. It's hard to look conspicuous in a fireman's outfit in a subdivision, and the hat was difficult to hide. The material of the coat was cheap and shiny like a Halloween costume and probably flammable.

Jeremy was a stripper and most of his gigs were at night. When he wasn't doing a bachelorette party, he stripped at a club downtown. I saw him infrequently, but sometimes he would get a night off, no other plans. On those evenings I would come home from work and find him sitting on the couch in jeans and a t-shirt, eating fried eggs or spaghetti and drinking beer. "Hey Mom," he would say. "I made eggs for you too. They're in the kitchen."

I want you to know this about my son: he cared about his mother. He did his own laundry; he cleaned up after himself. Before moving back in with me, he lived in Niagara Falls and he would call every Sunday evening. The only Sunday he missed was when he got into the fight and was stuck in the hospital with a broken ankle and a concussion. When he did get around to calling me, it was Tuesday and the first thing he said was, "I'm sorry I didn't call you sooner."

It's not something to be taken for granted to have a son who cares. When Fred's mother, Edna, was alive, he used to call her maybe once or twice a month. She lived in Buffalo, only an hour-and-a-half away from us in Toronto, but still far enough that she couldn't invite us for dinner after work or drop by unannounced. I was usually the one to suggest that he make the call, and he did it reluctantly, not because he didn't love her, but because he didn't understand why this love had to manifest itself through telephone calls. For him it was enough that he thought of her, that he had a visit planned in a few weeks. It never occurred to him that his mother could miss him or be lonely for his voice.

When I was pregnant and found out that my baby would be a boy, I cried. Fred didn't understand why I was already sad that the baby, the barely human wisp swimming in my belly, would grow up and forget me, find it a chore to simply call and tell me how he was doing. A daughter, I thought, wouldn't do that. But a son? It was inevitable. Pregnancy was making me sensitive, but beyond that mess of hormones I was sincerely scared about what it would be like to raise a boy.

When Edna died, Fred, Jeremy and I drove down to Buffalo in a snowstorm to attend the funeral. Jeremy was fifteen and Fred and I were still a few years away from our divorce. During the service I scanned the church and was surprised by how many people had shown up in spite of the weather. We'd met some of these people individually over the years, but to see them assembled in a group was a revelation. Edna had a son in a different city and a dead husband, but she'd rallied a community around her after the men had left: her bridge club, her fellow food bank volunteers, her coworkers from the library, neighbours, even grocery store employees. And they knew her so well, better than I knew her. "I found her favourite flowers," her Aquafitness instructor told me and handed over a bouquet of daffodils. I didn't know Edna had any particular affinity for daffodils. I grasped the bouquet and inhaled its earthy smell. The mustiness of the funeral parlour made me queasy and I held on to the flowers like a shot of something strong, carrying it with me for the rest of the afternoon. I'd been to my own parents' funerals, but Edna's felt different, more instructional than mournful, like I should pay attention and learn from it rather than participate in the grief. I brought the bouquet of daffodils with me back to the car and the wet snow clung to the petals. For a few moments it was beautiful and shimmery yellow.

When Fred and I divorced, I remembered Edna's funeral and wondered whether or not I would be able to build up a crowd like hers, stand-ins for her real family. Fred was going to remarry and move across town, but he might as well have moved across the country. Our divorce wasn't bitter, but I knew he wouldn't call me again. Jeremy already lived in Niagara Falls. I kept the house and the car, but I didn't have a bridge club and I'd never volunteered at a food bank. The house was profoundly silent.

My sister lived in Halifax, and when Fred told me he was leaving me, she suggested that I move out East to be near her. She offered to find me an apartment and a job. She'd moved away when she got married and it was fifteen years since we'd lived in the same city. I thought seriously about going, but I was more accustomed to my life in Toronto than being near her. So, I stayed at the house, alone, and just when I felt fear creeping up on me, Jeremy began calling regularly to make sure I was okay. "Hanging in there, Mom?" he asked, not too often, but enough to know that he worried. Every time the phone rang on a Sunday night, I would feel grateful, so overwhelmed with love for him.

Jeremy moved back in with me after the fight in Niagara Falls. He didn't give me many details about it, but it had been over Laura. He lived with her on the American side. He first met Laura when he was only thirteen years old on a visit to Edna's in Buffalo. Edna hosted an annual Fourth of July barbecue, and one of her food bank volunteer friends had brought her daughter along. Laura had straight blonde hair and green eyes. She had a brittle skinniness that she never grew out of, tomboyish as a child, but enviable as a young woman. The day of the picnic I could tell Jeremy liked her by the way he talked to her. He was still young enough that he hadn't learned how to hide the awed, dumbstruck look of a new crush. Laura was also thirteen, but she was more mature than him and reacted to his clumsy flirting with something haughtier and nonchalant. I noticed this and then I let it go, forgetting how powerful it is when you combine that kind of naïve love with the first inklings of adolescence. I didn't think I had anything to worry about: it was a sunny summer day and I was surrounded by my family, holding a cold beer, smelling freshly mowed grass. Everything radiated joy, but I only appreciated it later.

Jeremy and Laura saw each other whenever Jeremy was in town visiting his grandmother and sometimes he would go down on his own. I didn't discourage their relationship—it was innocent. Saturday afternoon matinees, meetings in the food court at the mall. Fred referred to Laura as Jeremy's "Buffalo girlfriend," as if our son had a string of them in different cities across North America.

After Edna died Jeremy still asked us to bring him to Buffalo. That Jeremy pursued Laura so doggedly always surprised me. I knew there were girls interested in him at home because they would call and I could practically hear them blush when they asked for him, but he longed only for Laura. He ran up long-distance phone bills sneaking calls to her at night until Fred noticed and disconnected the phone in his room. I never wished for a passionate love affair for my son. I'd hoped for him to find something more practical, something that could flourish and grow rather than sizzle and fade out.

The day after Jeremy graduated from high school he told us he was moving to Niagara Falls in September to live with Laura. He had American citizenship through Fred and I'd wanted him to use it for something more spectacular: an Ivy League school, maybe six months in Alaska. I didn't believe he was really going until he showed me that he'd saved all his money from his part-time jobs. He moved and soon after that Fred left and everyone was gone. That's when I thought about Edna again and wondered how she'd done it.

Jeremy started stripping in Niagara Falls, I knew that much. There weren't many job opportunities and he needed money to pay the rent. Laura was in college and she worked part-time at a bar, but it wasn't enough. He had other options, and said he started stripping as a joke, for laughs, but then he actually earned a decent living. Jeremy was a good-looking boy. He got it from Fred. He was pretty as a child, matching his good looks with muscles as he grew older, but I never imagined it would lead to that kind of career. He continued stripping when he moved back to Toronto, after his cast was removed. At first he told me he was a bartender and I had no reason to doubt him. He told me the truth when he started doing bachelorette parties and had to leave the house in costume. The parties paid better, and he needed more money if he wanted to move out. The evening he told me about stripping he was already wearing the policeman uniform.

"I see," I said after he explained. "Why?"

"I don't know," he said. "The money's good. It's fun."

"Do you have to dance?" I wanted to know if he was being paid to have sex, but I couldn't bring myself to ask.

"Yes, Mom, strippers dance."

"I didn't know you could dance." I couldn't even remember the last time I saw him dance. I didn't understand how stripping could be fun and I wondered if it was an offence to impersonate a police officer.

He held his cap in one hand. "Mom, it's okay. It's legal."

"Do you use your real name?"

He hesitated and told me he had a stage name. "I go under Mike Love."

"Like the singer in the Beach Boys?" I asked, confused, but relieved that he wasn't using his real name, that it couldn't be recognized by anyone we knew.

"The Beach Boys? I thought I made it up."

"Silly," I said to him. "He's the skinny one with the lovely voice." I couldn't stop myself from laughing and he smiled too and, I couldn't deny it, Jeremy was handsome in the uniform, with that smile of his. Mike Love wasn't a bad name for a stripper: there was something solid about it, tender instead of lewd. I was surprised that no one had ever pointed it out, not his boss or a customer, but he said he had a coworker named Elvis, so maybe it wasn't unusual to name yourself after a singer.

The next morning while I was driving to work a Beach Boys song came on the radio. The voices in harmony were sweet and simple, the sound of a sunny day. They were singing a song about a girl in love with the wrong kind of boy. Such normal problems. *Fun, fun, fun*, but only up until a point.

In the car I was scared for Jeremy, panicked that he was now in too deep, past the kinds of every day problems that could be sung about so breezily and innocently. I wondered if I could've done something to prevent this outcome, if I should've been more persistent about him staying away from Laura when he was younger. It was his relationship with her that led him to this life. Fred and I were going through our divorce when they were spending the most amount of time together, and maybe I'd been too distracted to pick up on warning signs that something unhealthy was developing.

It's crushing to be disappointed in your child because you can't help but feel like you've also failed. A double whammy. So, I tried to separate the sexual aspect of Jeremy's work from what he was doing, but this didn't amount to much more than being left with a stage name and some costumes. I imagined Jeremy was like the magician Fred and I had hired for his sixth birthday. The man had shown up on time with a duffel bag, some props, done his routine quickly, but effectively, collected payment and left, leaving a trail of children in his wake, all of them awestruck, hopped-up on sugar and wonder. There was a kind of power in that performance. Jeremy was powerful, too, but it was different from the power of a businessman or police officer or fireman. A magician. I could accept that.

When Jeremy moved to Niagara Falls, I was prepared for his departure as much as any mother can be prepared for their child moving out. I took a deep breath, cried a little and watched him leave. But, the second time he moved out was swifter. There was no sign it was coming. After he told me he was stripping, our lives fell into a steady pattern. Because Jeremy worked nights, I often went days without seeing him, only being aware of his existence by cereal bowls in the sink or a new pile of folded laundry by the machine.

He left a note, but I'd assumed it was a grocery list, so it sat there for a day until I picked it up. I was on my way out the door to buy a roast from the store. Jeremy didn't tell me where he was going, but he wrote, *Thank you for letting me stay here. I'll call. Love you,* as if I'd done him a favour by allowing him to move back in. I looked in his bedroom and most of his clothes were gone. He had really left.

He didn't call that night and I didn't know what to do. I should've been prepared for this—I knew him living with me again was only temporary—but I still couldn't believe it had happened so quickly and without a proper goodbye. I even considered calling Fred and asking him for advice, but I knew he and Jeremy rarely spoke. I almost called many people, but in the end I didn't call anyone. After another four days I still hadn't heard from Jeremy and the stillness of the house rattled me. I got into the car and drove downtown. Maybe I could catch him at work, make sure everything was okay.

Jeremy's bar was on the second floor of a building off of Yonge Street and after I parked and walked towards it, I realized that I didn't want to go in. I didn't want to see him on stage or see people at the club. Even worse, what if he wasn't there? What would I do? I was worried about other things too, like what the place smelled like or what I would say to the bouncer at the door. Below the club at street level was a convenience store and a psychic. A woman sat at a desk in the window of the psychic's and talking to her seemed less intimidating than facing whatever was at the top of those stairs.

The door made a muted ringing sound when I opened it. "Hi," I said. "I'm looking for my son. Maybe you can help."

The woman got up and smoothed her sweater. "You're lucky I don't have any clients at the moment. Why don't we go into the back room." She pulled the curtain behind her. "My name's Christina. What's yours?"

"I'm not here for a consultation," I said. "I don't have to go in the back. I'm just wondering if you know anything about my son. He works upstairs. His name is Jeremy."

Christina sunk back into her chair, unimpressed. "There are a lot of boys who work upstairs," she said. "I don't know anyone named Jeremy."

"He also goes by Mike Love."

"Mike Love's your son?" Her body language changed and she was warmer, more open.

"Do you know him?"

"Of course I know Mike. He's sweet. Is he really missing?"

"He hasn't been home in a few days."

"He was here on Sunday. He used my phone to call Laura. I thought he was just heading down to Niagara Falls."

"Why was he using your phone?"

"I sometimes let the boys use my phone for emergencies. If I'm not busy, I don't mind having them around."

"He called Laura?" I asked. "Do you know her?"

"I don't, but Mike's told me about her."

It bothered me that Christina knew so much about Jeremy and yet insisted on calling him by his stage name. I'd been relieved by his stage name at first, but listening to Christina so brazenly call him something else offended me. I'd gone to a lot of trouble picking the right name for him. Jeremy was the name of my grandfather and my father's middle name. It was important, not something to be cast aside.

"What do you know about Laura?" I asked. I wondered if Christina really was psychic. She was in her mid-forties and wore too much makeup. Her nails were red and shiny and matched the velvet curtain behind her. She seemed tired, but maybe the burden of her psychic abilities was exhausting. All that otherworldly chatter piling up on top of the regular sounds of the city. I leaned on the counter and listened to her, but what she told me sounded more like gossip than prophecies.

"Laura's pregnant. She thinks it's Mike's baby. He's going to see her."

"Oh," I said. "Really?"

"You didn't know?"

"I knew," I lied. "I just wanted confirmation."

"No problem. Tell Mike to take care of himself. I don't know if I trust that Laura girl."

I left and stood outside on the sidewalk. I could hear music coming from the bar upstairs, just the thump of the beat, a low grumble of vibration, no actual melody. I walked back to the car and drove home, the downtown lights blinking and blurry. Radio off.

I shouldn't have been surprised that Jeremy was with Laura, but I was. During the fight in Niagara Falls, another man had punched him—Laura's new boyfriend maybe?—and as Jeremy had fallen, his foot twisted around a bar stool and snapped at the ankle. "I'm moving back," he told me after it happened. "Laura doesn't want to live with me anymore and I don't want to stay." He sounded so ashamed that I was certain the humiliation would override any desire to return in the future. I didn't think he'd seen her once since moving back.

I was the one who picked him up in Niagara Falls. He protested at first when I offered, said he would just take the bus, but he didn't try very hard to stop me. I didn't want him aggravating his leg getting to the station or falling asleep for too long with his concussion. I took a sick day at work and left first thing the next morning. There was no traffic on the QEW and the customs officer waved me through at the border. When I pulled into Jeremy's driveway, he came out right away, a bag slung on his shoulder, crutches propping him up. The cast was bigger than I'd imagined, off-white, as if he'd already gotten it dirty. He was almost twenty years old.

I got him settled in the back seat so that he could stretch out his leg. His face was swollen and he hadn't shaved in a few days.

"Where's Laura?" I asked.

"Not home," he said.

"Did you already say goodbye?"

"Kind of."

"Are you okay?"

"Yeah."

I pulled out of the driveway and asked if he minded if I stopped to look at the Falls. By his one-word answers I knew he wouldn't be interested in any last minute sightseeing, but now that he was safe with me, I was angry. He hadn't thanked me for coming and I wanted to do something for myself, something as compensation for the drive. I hadn't been in the area in years and I wondered if the scenery had changed at all. I drove through town and followed the signs while Jeremy remained sullen in the back. At the Falls, he refused to get out, so I stopped in a nearby hotel parking lot and left the car idling so that he wouldn't get cold.

It was late March and there was still some snow, but by the Falls everything was moist and wet. I wasn't wearing the right kind of shoes, and my heels sank into the ground. The area surrounding the Falls was empty and there were hardly any tourists. The souvenir shops were open, but their windows were steamed up and there was one lone vendor, a man selling samosas from a cart.

On the American side, the Falls aren't right in front of you the way they are in Canada. You have to crane your neck to see them. I saw more visitors as I approached the water, small clumps of people here and there huddled in groups, but there was enough space between us that I felt isolated from them. I couldn't even hear their voices. I wondered how amazing it must feel to be the only person around, if that was ever even possible. Maybe early, early morning, just at dawn. All sounds drowned out by the roar of the Falls. The mist settled in my hair and on my jacket and I could feel a thin film of water on my cheeks. I only stayed for a few minutes and then went back to the car. Jeremy had his eyes shut, but I knew he was awake.

"Did you come often to the Falls?" I asked.

"Nope." That was all he said. He kept his eyes closed.

"But they're so close to you." In retrospect I was even more disappointed by this than I'd been when he told me he was stripping. To have something so fantastic so close and ignoring it made me wonder if I'd ever taught him anything. "What happened, Jer?" I finally asked after we crossed the border. He didn't answer. He had dozed off, this time for real, and for the last hour of the trip I listened to the rhythmic pant of his snores.

As I drove home from the psychic, I tried to forget what she'd told me. Instead I thought about that day I picked Jeremy up in Niagara Falls, and I tried to recall the kind of lightness I felt while he slept in the backseat. I'd been frustrated, worried about him, but beyond that I was relieved that he hadn't told me what had happened with Laura. I was thankful for not being burdened by his problems. I couldn't blame myself for them if I didn't know what they were and there was nothing else I could do except be happy to have him with me again. I wondered if I had told myself to enjoy it, to cling to it for as long as I could, because by then I should've learned enough to know that it wouldn't last.

THE OCCULT

1. PALM READING

Try this: place your palm close to someone else's. Your hands should face each other, but not touch. Feel the heat radiate between the two of you. If you're lucky the warmth will be palpable. Comforting. Do you know what's happening? Your auras are conversing. A homeless man in Toronto taught this trick to Hannah a few days before she moved to Montreal. She'd given him a loonie, and then he walked beside her for the next block. She didn't want to be rude, so she spoke to him and uncomfortably held her hand close to his, and in the end she was happy for the tip. It was a good icebreaker at parties and she was going to need icebreakers soon. She quickly learned that some palms were hotter than others, some conversations stronger.

She met Eric a month after she moved and he countered with his own parlour trick, which was that he could read palms, or at least knew the names of the lines. They stood in a dark corner at the back of a bar and she offered him her hand. He pointed out the lines. *Your life line cups your thumb. The head line cuts across your palm. And,* he said pressing down gently, *your heart line is the one that curves up by your fingers.*

2. ASTROLOGY

Hannah is surprised but not surprised that she can't find a pregnancy test at the dep around the corner from her apartment. She has relied on this store for so many essentials: cheap wine, toilet paper, the occasional onion fished out from the dirty bin by the cash register. A pregnancy test is probably pushing it. It's mid-March and it's snowing outside, the millionth snowstorm of her first Montreal winter, and she reluctantly heads towards the nearest pharmacy four blocks away. She plucks a test from the harshly lit aisles and returns home, cold and wet and shivery.

Hannah pees on the stick and it turns pink. She's surprised but not surprised when she learns that pink means positive. (Does it also mean that the baby will be a girl? She reads the package and feels dumb when, obviously, it doesn't.)

Hannah paces around her apartment in her pyjamas, holds the stick and calculates. Nine months from now will be January, which means the baby will be a Capricorn. A friend had once offered to do her astrological chart, but she turned her down, so Hannah's only grasping at astrological clues. She's a Cancer and she knows that Capricorns don't mesh well with Cancers. Maybe astrology doesn't apply to mothers and their children?

Eric is an Aries. Hannah knows this because he'd mentioned that he and a friend were going to throw a joint birthday party at the beginning of April. After the third

time they'd slept together, he didn't call for eight days, and
then when they finally did talk, they didn't have much to
say to each other. Cancers aren't supposed to be compat-
ible with Aries either. Maybe astrology *was* right, maybe the
indicators were staring her plain in the face: the stars were
misaligned from the very beginning.

3. EXTRA-SENSORY PERCEPTION

Hannah wakes up early the next morning and goes to work.
Even before she's taken off her coat and unwound her scarf,
Dominique, who works in the cubicle next to hers, says,
"You don't look very happy today." Hannah keeps her toque
on and complains about how cold it is outside.

They work quietly until a window pops up on her screen
reminding her that there's going to be a baby shower for
their coworker, Sylvie, at lunch. Hannah wants to skip it,
but Dominique waits for her before leaving.

"There's going to be cake," she says, her voice sing-songy
and sweet, and Hannah can't say no.

The department congregates in the cafeteria. Everyone
lingers and takes turns touching Sylvie's belly.

"His foot's right here," Sylvie says and holds Dominique's
hand to it.

"I can feel it!" Dominique says. "Hannah, check this!"

Hannah shook Sylvie's hand when she first transferred
to the office, but they've never hugged, hardly talked, and
a touch like this seems too intimate for people who are
practically strangers, so she does it gingerly, awkwardly.
She probes the area for a knot of tissue, a baby's foot pressing against his mother's insides, but everything is smooth,
curved round, like a globe or a medicine ball.

"Oops," Sylvie says. "He moved. He's hiding from you."

Hannah backs up and helps herself to the grocery store cake, and when the baby starts to kick again, she holds up the plastic plate to show that her hands are full.

Back at her desk, she picks up the phone to call Eric. He doesn't answer so she leaves him a message, a neutral one. He calls back within ten minutes, but when she sees his name on her caller ID she ignores it. She listens to the message before going home for the evening and in it he reminds her of his birthday party. This weekend. *You can bring a friend if you want.*

4. EXORCISM

It's a relief to think of time in terms of distance, not growth. Hannah's driving to Toronto for the weekend and each hour that passes is another 120 kilometres. Before getting the abortion, she worried that for every minute that ticked by, the thing inside of her became more real. More defined. What was a cluster of cells one hour bloomed into an embryo the next and, if she waited another night, might be a fetus by daybreak. With a nose. Or maybe little feet that kicked. She knew it didn't work that way, that the chronology was more drawn out, but her pants seemed tighter.

The abortion didn't hurt the way Hannah was afraid it would and, either way, overriding the pain was a feeling of deep, exhausting relief. The trip to Toronto was a week later and because it coincided with her grandfather's birthday, she was hesitant to cancel. Her hormones were still out of whack and she cried in the car. Once. She'd taken a detour from the monotony of the highway and was driving on a stretch outside of Kingston that passed through the Thousand Islands. It gave way to a more gentle and scenic view, the St. Lawrence hugging the curve of the road. She'd visited the area one summer, stayed with a childhood friend who had a cottage on one of the tiny islands. She remembers the two of them pushing a canoe into the water, her oar slicing through the calm, clear river.

In the early spring the scenery is desolate. The water is grey-white and icy and the solitary houses on the small islands shuttered and empty. As she merges back on to the 401, she snuffles, stops crying, takes a big, gulping breath. But it was a good kind of cry. Things could've turned out so much worse.

5. PROPHECIES

Hannah was nineteen years old at the end of 1999, working at a grocery store when she wasn't in school. People would come in and buy ten-pound sacks of flour, flats of water bottles and dozens of double D batteries, all in preparation for Y2K and the possibility of ultimate world destruction. These were people who'd read a sidebar in the newspaper about what items to have on hand in an emergency and wanted to stock up, but sometimes they would also get the crazies, people who gripped her arm desperately and wheezed, "Where's the bottled water? I want *all of it.*" There was something vaguely prophetic about their hysteria and sometimes Hannah would even find herself in a minor panic.

New Year's Eve approached and Hannah thought that if the world ended, she wouldn't be surprised. It would make sense if it did. Still, she didn't make special plans for this potential last day of Earth. On December 31st she sat in her boyfriend's basement apartment with a few of their friends. They drank wine and she doesn't remember what they talked about. When midnight struck, she squeezed her eyes shut and wondered if anything would be different when she opened them again. But everything was fine! The world didn't fall apart; the computers kept running. They toasted each other, drank more wine, went to bed by three. She got the feeling that they were disappointed that nothing more spectacular had happened.

While in Toronto, Hannah visits this ex-boyfriend briefly. He has a new place, no longer a mouldy basement, now a postage-stamp sized condo downtown, all granite and glass. If the apocalypse loomed again, she wouldn't choose to spend it with him, but she's feeling nostalgic and decides that an hour while she's visiting the city is fair.

He asks her how she's doing, but he asks with a certain inflection—"how are you *doing*?"—as if he's genuinely concerned, like maybe he suspects something's wrong. Hannah keeps looking at herself in the mirror and wondering if she looks different. She's worried that her eyes look older or sad or that, even if she looks the same, maybe her palms give off less heat after such a cold winter.

As they're talking, it starts raining and Hannah pauses to listen to it beat against his windows. The thought of rain is appealing and she hopes the weather is the same in Montreal. Rain would melt the snow, clean the streets.

"I'm good." She says it confidently and he believes her, which is satisfying enough. Maybe "good" isn't the right word to describe how she feels, but while she's sitting there she realizes that she does feel differently than she has in a long time. She feels impermeable.

6. SIGNS

When Hannah leaves her ex-boyfriend's condo, she sees a rainbow stretching somewhere in the distance towards the lake. She stands underneath an awning and stares at it. The colours are blurred and faint, but it's definitely a rainbow.

Logically, rationally and scientifically, she knows that a rainbow is just the reflection of light on water droplets. But she knows lots of things. She also knows that palm reading is a fluke and astrology can be interpreted any way one wants. She knows that she can't read minds and people can't read hers, and that the end of the world will probably not happen on the day everyone is predicting. Most of all she knows that life just *happens* and that there isn't an overarching, sensible pattern to it, but it doesn't mean that she can't believe in signs or look to them for guidance.

The rainbow, Hannah decides, as she walks to the subway, is a good sign. She's not sure what else it could be.

ART HISTORY

THERE'S A SEGMENT OF THE POPULATION that even when forced will not throw out their useless and worthless belongings. My parents got rich by capitalizing on this sentimental weakness. They started by renting out 5x10 foot cubes that could be filled with detritus and stored in a warehouse, We Store, out of sight and out of mind. They opened another warehouse with more storage options and as the condo industry boomed, their business flourished. They now own a series of We Stores scattered around the Greater Toronto Area, all of them close to capacity and stuffed to the gills with—despite their owners' claims—crap. Sometimes an expensive piece of antique furniture will come in for storage, something that can't possibly match its owner's new seven hundred square foot minimalist condo, but in general We Store houses garage sale fare—stained couches, plastic bags of greying stuffed animals, boxes of mismatched cutlery—

everything packed carefully and precisely, as if their owners were historians preserving the most valuable of artifacts.

During high school I spent my summers working in reception at the warehouse in Mississauga, a half-hour drive from our home in Toronto. This particular We Store was wedged between the highway and a vast field that hadn't yet been developed into an industrial park or subdivision. At dusk if I stood at the edge of the parking lot with my back to the warehouse and the highway, I could almost trick myself into thinking I was in the country, that hum of crickets and mosquitoes, all that overgrown former farmland bleached pale green and yellow from the summer sun. And there were animals too, small ones, raccoons and skunks and foxes, that would emerge from the field and nose their way towards the garbage bins. The unlucky ones would wander off and get slammed by cars that took the highway exit too quickly. We were the closest building, so the corpses often got tossed on our property, glassy-eyed and bloody, their fur still soft. My father once found a dead deer behind the garbage bins. It must have dragged itself over, looking for a place to die with dignity.

The summer I was seventeen, my older sister Greta asked our parents to get her boyfriend a job at one of the warehouses. Daniel was about to start a master's degree in art history and the gallery he was supposed to work at closed at the last minute. He needed the money, so my father hired him and placed him as the assistant to our full-time facilities manager, Gord. Daniel was stationed in Mississauga with me.

On his first day at We Store there was mass carnage: an entire family of raccoons, two big ones and two little ones, done in by a transport truck. Their bodies were splayed across the parking lot, and I had to swerve to avoid them when I pulled in that morning. Daniel arrived soon afterwards.

"Hey April," he said when he saw me. "It's pretty gross out there." I knew one of his responsibilities would be to clean it up, but I waited for Gord to break the news to him.

"How exactly do I get rid of them?" Daniel asked. He tried to be cheerful about it. "I wasn't told this job required a rabies shot."

Gord held out a pair of gloves and a garbage bag and handed them over. "It was a full moon last night; we always get casualties on full moons. A few weeks ago it was skunks. Where the hell do skunks come from?"

"I've never really thought about it," Daniel said.

"It's too bad the racoons landed in the parking lot. If they get killed in the street the city will take care of them."

"Maybe I can ask them nicely."

"You'll have to clean the bodies quick before they start to rot. And do the babies first; they bother the customers."

"I'm sorry," I said to Daniel from where I sat at reception. He snapped on the gloves and headed outside.

"I've never been spoiled," Greta said to Mom that night. She'd driven over from the apartment she shared with Daniel downtown. The three of us had dinner together while Dad worked late.

"Okay," Mom said.

"I mean, I've never bothered you and Dad for anything extravagant or crazy, right? Neither has April. We just weren't raised like that."

"Sure," Mom looked at me and I shrugged.

"So, I know it was a lot asking you to give Daniel a job at the last minute, but I don't know why you had to give him *that* job."

"Is it bad?"

"Yes."

"Is it that bad, April?" Mom and Greta turned and stared at me.

"Kind of," I said. "He spent the morning scrubbing road-kill off the parking lot."

"See, it's a shitty job. I'm sorry, but it is."

"Isn't art working with your hands?"

"Mom, he's studying art history. He doesn't *use his hands*."

"He can quit if he doesn't like it."

"Can you talk to Dad about it?"

Mom agreed to, but even if she did, Daniel's position didn't change. He didn't quit in protest either. He showed up every morning on time and did whatever Gord told him to do, although I got the feeling he stuck it out to prove a point to either Greta or my parents.

Daniel was more useful, or at least sturdier than Phillip, last summer's maintenance assistant. Phillip's mother worked in accounting and had pulled some strings to get him on-board. He was nineteen, geeky and awkward, and his parents were worried that he spent too much time in front of the computer. They encouraged a summer foray into manual labour thinking it would be a good character building experience, if not a muscle building one. Phillip and I were the youngest people at the warehouse and became friends when Gord asked me to show him where to find the lawn mower. Phillip's clumsiness pained him. "I just can't stand to look at his face again today," Gord said, not even apologetically. Whenever Gord became too fed up, Phillip would lay low and sit with me in reception. One afternoon we snuck away to an empty storage room to smoke a joint he'd supposedly brought to work.

"So, where is it?" I asked. I'd smoked pot once, but hadn't inhaled properly and only felt a keen awareness of my own sobriety. I was excited to smoke up with him and knew that I wouldn't be embarrassed if I coughed too much or said something dumb. Phillip squirmed and admitted he didn't have one. "I just wanted to get you alone," he said looking down. His skinniness made me feel fierce and so I leaned over and kissed him and we made out on the cold, concrete floor, the sickly fluorescent lights betraying the real summer sun outside. After that we used his keys to open storage cubes and make out behind stacks of boxes or on plastic covered couches. No one ever caught us.

Phillip was fired before the summer even ended when he knocked over a jug of paint solvent. The chemicals seeped under the door of a storage locker and corroded a chunk of a rattan chair. He called me at reception a few times after he left, but outside the confines of the warehouse he lost his sheen.

I'd only been working a week when Daniel started, but I already hated being there. I dealt with customers occasionally, but I resented them, annoyed by the fact that they chose to spend money to keep their ugly, cheap belongings when they could donate them or simply throw them out. I imagined that all of those useless, unused items languishing in row after row of storage lockers weighed heavy on the world, that we were saddling it with too much unnecessary burden. There had to be some kind of physical impact; I worried we would throw the earth off its orbit.

I was going to quit. I practiced the speech I would give to my parents while I sat at reception, staring at the phone and wondering when it would ring. It was a moral stance, I would tell them. Not that I found them or their business immoral (I was grateful for what their entrepreneurship had provided our family), but I didn't want to willingly participate in the perpetuation of blind consumption. Or something. I chickened out. Greta had also worked at We Store in high school and had emerged unscathed. Finally, to appease myself, I developed a theory. I rationalized that I was entitled to specific amounts of things in my life, that there was a finite limit to love and good fortune. By the same logic, the more I chipped away at the bad stuff, the less I would have to endure in the future. This is how I felt about my boredom at We Store: if I could get it out of the way—the tedium of an office job—there would be more room left in the rest of my life for something more exciting, more vibrant. I tried to derive a kind of pleasure from the mindless work, a satisfaction of paying my dues. I typed letters, I answered phones and felt efficient and purposefully bored.

Then Daniel started working and things got more interesting. He and Greta had been dating for two years, but I knew him only as an extension of my sister. My awareness of him was coloured entirely by his relationship to her and it was strange talking to him at We Store as if he was a real person, not just a character in my sister's life.

Daniel and I talked a lot because neither of us had much to do. We knew we were only there thanks to nepotism; I doubt Dad would have hired strangers to do our jobs if we left. After the first week of consistent conversation, I was surprised by how much I liked Daniel. He was funny in a way I had never noticed before, and smart.

Daniel took walks whenever there was a lull in his day. He would cut through the field towards the closest strip mall. I would see him sometimes emerge from the tall grass, swatting away mosquitoes, carrying two chocolate Frosties from Wendy's—one for him, one for me. Everyone else drove to the strip mall. "It's exercise," he said.

Daniel also lectured me about art, practice for his future career as an art history professor. He explained chronologically, skipping from Rococo to Romanticism. "It's not so bad working here," he once told me. "I'm going through a Cubist phase anyway."

A large part of my job consisted of printing out and mailing renewal notices. People often lost track of their storage space and treated it as they would a musty basement, forgetting that these spaces were run by people who had their credit card numbers and charged interest. After labelling a new batch of notices, a girl approached my desk and asked for the biggest storage space she could get.

Her name was Maggie and she was different than our usual customers. She was young, about Greta's age, and pretty. I took her outside to the back where there was a row of small sheds, all of them lined with identical white vinyl siding and shuttered with orange metal doors. From far away they looked like their own little subdivision, uniformly symmetric, little boxes made of ticky-tacky. There was even a row of flowers planted around the edges. Daniel watered them every day. My father advertised them as "cottages," but I couldn't bring myself to call them that. I opened the door and showed her the space.

"This is 10x30 feet, enough for a three to four bedroom home. You can fit appliances and like, patio furniture in it."

"Is there electricity?" she asked.

"Some units have it. It costs extra."

"It's perfect," she breathed. "I'll take it."

Maggie returned the next day with a U-Haul. I was curious about what she needed the storage space for. I imagined her as the type who bought around-the-world plane tickets and needed to store her quirky, vintage belongings while she sublet her loft. She had a girlfriend with her and the two of them worked quickly, hauling out boxes and a rolled-up rug. The only item they had trouble with was a couch, dark brown and corduroy. Daniel helped them with that.

I only worked Wednesday to Friday, relieving the regular receptionist so she could spend extra time with her children. When I returned the following Wednesday I was surprised to see Maggie again. She walked across the parking lot with a cup of coffee. I followed her and noticed that she'd gone into her storage shed and closed the door behind her. After sending out a few renewal notices, I went outside and knocked on her door. She opened it a crack. When she saw me, she opened the door wider and I peeked inside. The entire cube looked like a living room. The couch was pushed along the far wall and a coffee table cut the room in half. The rug, blue and white striped, was rolled out underneath.

"Hey," she said. "What's up?"

"Do you live here?" I asked.

"Not exactly."

"You're not allowed to live here."

"I know," she said. "Don't worry, I'm not. Come in. Your name's April, right? Are you just working here for the summer?"

I didn't answer. "I'm not sure what you're doing." I said instead, my voice stumbling.

"Will you get me in trouble if I tell you?" I shook my head.

"I'm a photographer primarily, but this is a conceptual art piece. I'm pretending to live here and I'm documenting it. The couch folds out into a bed, but I've only spent the night once. It's creepy here at night, so I've been coming mostly during the day."

Conceptual art. Daniel hadn't gotten to that one yet. "What do you mean an art piece? Why?"

"It's part of my MFA thesis. I'm not allowed to do this, am I?"

"I don't think so," I said.

"It's just for a month. As long as the owner doesn't find out, I'll be fine."

"He won't," I promised, even though she didn't know the owners were my parents.

"This place is pretty cozy, isn't it?"

As she pointed out more decorating details, Daniel came to the doorway holding my daily Frosty. Maggie had forgotten to close the door all the way and he saw us when he cut through the field.

"Hi?" He peered into the shed and Maggie suddenly looked nervous.

"Don't worry," I said. "Daniel's studying art history. He'll keep quiet." I felt important as I reassured her, in on something big. I took the cup out of his hand and spooned up some ice cream.

The next time I saw Maggie she was outside behind the row of sheds setting up a tripod.

"Hey April," she asked. "Can I take your picture?"

"Me?"

"It would be great if I got photos of the people who work here," she said. "You don't have to if you're not comfortable."

But I agreed, flattered that she wanted to use me in her thesis. She directed me to look up at the sky. I threw my head back and as I waited for her to take my picture, I noticed how big the sky was out here. There weren't any tall buildings to block the sky's hugeness, no houses either. This surprised me the way you're surprised when you discover something obvious: of *course* the sky was bigger out here, of *course* it would be this beautiful. As Maggie fiddled with the camera, I stared at the wisps of clouds and blue sky, its beauty set inside a grid of power lines.

I mentioned the photos to Daniel, and he told me that Maggie had taken his photo too.

"What are you doing in your photo?" I asked.

"Watering the flowers."

This made me laugh. I wasn't sure if he was lying.

"I look like the little girl in that Renoir painting."

"Renoir?"

"April," Daniel said. "I have so much to teach you."

I let him use my computer to find an image of it online. The painting was of a smiling little girl holding a watering can, all dreamy brush strokes and shades of pastel.

"Were you wearing a dress too?" I asked.

"Of course," he said. "Anything for art."

Later that afternoon things were slow, so when Daniel was about to leave to get Frosties, I decided I'd go with him. I was still feeling high off the photo shoot with Maggie that morning.

Daniel was surprised when I ran up behind him. The walk was longer than I expected and blades of crab grass scratched my ankles.

"I can't believe you do this every day," I complained. "It's so hot out. My head is overheating, feel it." He placed his palm on the top of my head. I had dark hair and in the summer it soaked up heat if I wasn't wearing a hat.

"Jesus, you're burning up."

I reached up and touched his head too, pressing my fingers into his sandy coloured short hair. It was much cooler than mine. We kept walking and for a few moments he kept his hand on my head, protecting it from the sun.

Daniel and I decided not to tell anyone about Maggie. We knew that if she got in trouble, her whole project would be ruined. He and Greta would sometimes come over for dinner and there would be no talk of art students or photography. Every so often my parents or Greta asked us about work at the warehouse. "It's not so bad," I would say and Daniel would agree and then we would smile at each other quickly. I savoured the secret between us, proof of our strengthening bond.

With Maggie spending her days at We Store, work took on a different rhythm. My days of answering the telephone or stuffing envelopes were punctuated not only by the occasional art lecture from Daniel, but by visits with Maggie as well. She was discreet, but often stopped by reception to say hello. She invited me over for a drink once, and after I sat down took a bottle of lemonade out of the bar fridge she'd plugged into the corner of the shed. She had a laptop propped up on the table and would spend hours in there typing. Daniel liked talking to Maggie too, and sometimes I would see them hanging out behind her shed. Occasionally I would join them, but in general we socialized in pairs: me and Daniel, me and Maggie, or Maggie and Daniel.

One day I drove to Wendy's to buy the Frosties, and I even picked one up for Maggie, whose car I'd seen in the parking lot. It was a hot day and I welcomed the cool blast of air conditioning. When I returned I couldn't find Daniel, so I knocked on Maggie's shed first and waited for her to answer. Daniel was there with her, sitting on the couch. "Good timing," I said, walked in and perched on the edge of the coffee table holding the tray of cups. "It's so hot in here. I don't know how you can get any work done. You'll need this."

Maggie took her Frosty first. Daniel didn't look at me when I passed his over.

"Are you okay?" I asked him. "You look weird."

His cheeks were rosy and sweaty from the heat. Maggie laughed and Daniel smiled at her, but it wasn't the wry smile he gave me when we joked around at reception; it was more private. There was something about the smile that reminded me of my previous summer. I remembered Phillip and me inside the suffocating storage cubes, the privacy they afforded. We could close the door behind us and it was like we had stepped into a vacuum; no one had any idea where we were or what we were doing. A minute or an hour would pass and nothing would change, not even the shadows.

I walked back to reception and for the first time I wondered if Maggie and Daniel were doing the same thing. It hadn't occurred to me earlier, and I didn't think they could be, but I wasn't sure. When Daniel came by my desk later that afternoon, I was still unsettled.

"Is something going on between you and Maggie?" I asked. It just came out.

"Listen," he said. "Don't tell Greta about any of this."

"What's that supposed to mean?"

"Let me talk to her, okay, April? It's complicated." He

talked to me like I was a child or a little sister. I felt my eyes well up and I looked down at my keyboard.

"I can't believe it." I said.

"Hey," he said. "It'll be okay." He briefly touched the top of my head, like he had that day out in the sun. I hadn't accompanied him on his walks since then. I was waiting for him to ask me first, as if it would be more appropriate that way, but he never did. I sometimes found myself feeling embarrassed for hoping that he would ask and then for thinking that if I invited myself it could be construed as inappropriate. What was inappropriate about it? I shook his hand away.

Maybe this was the real reason we didn't talk about Maggie around Greta. It had nothing to do with putting her thesis project in jeopardy or because Daniel and I shared a secret. It was, I suppose, because he had his own secret. I added up the clues: Daniel's art lectures had tapered off and were sloppy as he meandered through Surrealism. Recently I was the one making the Frosty runs. Daniel no longer had any lulls in his days.

"I have work to do," I said to him.

I couldn't believe that I hadn't noticed anything between Maggie and Daniel sooner. That Daniel could be cheating on Greta was beyond me, not an event I had planned on working into my theory of why I was still there at We Store. Did this count as something bad for me or just for Greta? More for Greta, but I still felt gutted, my cheeks hot with shame or anger, I wasn't sure which.

I saw the fallacy of my theory. I wasn't chipping away at my lifetime supply of tedium. I was being cushioned by it. Boredom bred boredom, and even worse, made you accustomed to it. The previous summer I had had Phillip to distract me, and this summer I had Daniel for awhile, but now that I suspected something going on between him and Maggie, all I had was a glaring reminder of my own naivety.

I shut off the computer and went outside for air. I leaned against my car and sipped the remains of the Frosty. It was warm by then, liquefied and sickly syrupy. I faced away from the storage sheds and thought about what I was going to do.

Before I did anything definitive—told Gord about Maggie, told Greta about Daniel, told my parents that I was going to quit—or worse, before I did absolutely nothing, I looked up at the sky, still big, still blue. I could see the moon, its white, craggy outline far off in the horizon. I forgot you could sometimes see the moon in the daytime. It wasn't a full moon, but it was almost there.

I thought of the animals living out in the field, all those doomed rodents, invisible until they were found dead on the side of the road or smeared on our parking lot. I hoped that they would come out that night in a moonlit stupor and sacrifice themselves so that Daniel would be forced to scrub the guts and hearts and bones from the asphalt in the sweltering, suburban summer heat. If this happened, my theory could possibly be redeemed. I felt good thinking and hoping for it, standing there, my legs burning against the side of my car while I clutched that dripping milkshake.

HUSHPUPPIES

DAY 1: BOUGHT A ROAD ATLAS AND SOME BAD COFFEE.

Thomas picked Nikki up from the subway station. It was late afternoon and she was standing out front with her sunglasses on, clutching her bags, ready. She threw her things into the back seat of his car and jumped into the front. They'd saved up some money and were going on vacation. Skipping town.

Thomas drove until just before Windsor where they stopped at a Tim Hortons so Nikki could take the wheel. He said he got nervous at the border, that customs officers were nicer to girls anyway. The traffic was bad heading into Detroit and Nikki got nervous on the bridge. She didn't drive often, and they were so high up, only a frothy brown strip of water separating the two cities below them. When they crossed into Michigan there was construction on the highways and half the time they were forced to drive on the shoulder, on the rumble strips—those grooves on the side of the highway that are there to remind you when you're veering off course.

They drove until midnight. When they were too tired to go any further, they pulled off at the next exit. Piqua, Ohio. The pamphlet Nikki grabbed from the motel lobby advertised only churches, a dozen of them. She hadn't expected that many for what seemed like a small town, and she took this as a sign that they were in a different country, that this was the kind of thing that separated Canada from the United States. She was so eager to feel far away that she kept grasping at signs that things were different. This was something.

It took ten minutes for the owner of the motel to wake up and when they got their room, they noticed a tiny hole drilled just above the headboard facing the full-length mirror. It reminded Nikki of a news segment she'd seen about motels installing video cameras, filming their customers having sex and then distributing the footage on the Internet. She stuffed a wad of toilet paper into the hole.

Nikki ran out to get her toothbrush from the car and noticed a cornfield backing onto the parking lot. There were little clouds of fireflies darting around in crazy circles. She would've gone closer to look at them, but the cornfield looked ominous and huge, darker than the sky, like it could swallow her whole.

In the morning they followed the state line, entered Kentucky, dipped into Indiana. They drove through a county called Little Switzerland that was all lush, rolling hills and A-frame houses. They bought coffee from a general store and drank it in the parking lot. Nikki suggested they just stop here, buy an A-frame and settle forever. They leaned against the car, breathed, squinted at the hills, but didn't stay.

When they got to Nashville it was dark. Their motel was cornered in-between two highways, one to Memphis and one to Knoxville. They sat on the steps, their backs to the road, and shared a cigarette.

"I'm going to write a poem about this." Thomas said. He dropped the cigarette. The tip glowed. "And I never write poetry."

Nikki leaned against him and looked up. "I know what you mean."

DAY 3: DROVE BY A FIELD OF DEER. I TRIED TO COUNT THEM, BUT THERE WERE TOO MANY. THEY LOOKED AT US AND THEN SAUN-TERED AWAY.

Nikki met Thomas that spring when he was finishing school. He was studying photography and described his latest project to her.

"I'm taking photos of people standing in the financial district surrounded by buildings on a Sunday when there's no one around. And then I take another picture of them in the same pose, but standing in a field somewhere outside the city."

"That's an interesting juxtaposition," Nikki said to him. She thought he was cute.

"I need more models."

They met a week later on a Sunday at nine in the morning at the foot of a skyscraper, First Canadian Place. The area outside was empty, not one businessman around, and she could see their wobbly reflections in the shiny dark glass of the buildings. She wore black pants, a black t-shirt and pink flip-flops. Thomas didn't want the flip-flops in the photo, so she posed barefoot. The cement was cold. He wanted the same light for the second picture, so the next day he picked her up at the same time and they drove out of the city. West and then north. It was strip mall, subdivision, subdivision, strip mall, farm, strip mall, country. They listened to Neil Young and drank Coke he kept in a cooler in the trunk. When he found the field he wanted to photograph, they hopped a barbed wire fence and started walking.

After the pictures they kissed in the field. That spring Toronto was infested with ladybugs, and Nikki saw them everywhere, swarming benches and poles, flying slowly and getting stupidly tangled up in hair or in folds of clothing. After they kissed Nikki forgot all about the infestation and when she looked down and noticed a tiny red ladybug crawling on her big toe she thought, *how special.*

Thomas lived in an apartment off of College Street just east of Dufferin. June kicked off with a heat wave and the two of them spent nights laying naked on his bed, the television on mute in the corner, an electric fan whirring and blowing cool air onto the soles of their feet. It was too hot to be close, but they were giddy enough to have sex anyway, sweaty before they even touched. They drank his roommate's cold white wine because he always kept a bottle in the fridge while theirs would still be wrapped in the paper bag, forgotten in the corner.

There was something about that summer, the heat. Nikki was twenty-one when it started and twenty-two when it ended and she kept lists of the places where she and Thomas had sex. Mostly his apartment. Once, High Park. After they left she just wrote, *everywhere.*

DAY 5: PICKED UP WOOD FOR A FIRE. IT COST THREE DOLLARS, BUT THERE WAS NO ONE AROUND TO COLLECT THE MONEY, JUST SOME ENVELOPES. I PUT THE MONEY IN AN ENVELOPE AND SLID

IT UNDER THE OFFICE DOOR. THOUGHT ABOUT NOT PAYING, BUT
THERE ARE PLACES TO BE CHEAP, AND SOMEONE WENT TO A LOT
OF TROUBLE BUNDLING UP THE WOOD.

Nikki's brother didn't know she was gone until he called
her cell phone a few days later. She and Thomas had made
their way to the Smoky Mountains at the edge of Tennessee.
Her brother was in Toronto, visiting from out-of-town. Had
Nikki forgotten that he was supposed to stay with her that
weekend? She had. The reception on her phone was bad so
she walked to the only pay phone on site and called him back.

"I'm sorry," she said. "I'm in the Smoky Mountains."

"What are you talking about?" Her brother was outside
her apartment building.

"You didn't call me before you left." Nikki said. "You
should've reminded me."

"The Smoky Mountains?"

"Tennessee. I'm with Thom."

"What the hell?" he asked. "Why are you in Tennessee?"

"I'm on vacation. I didn't tell you I was going?"

"Where am I supposed to stay?"

"I'm sorry," she said again.

When Nikki was younger she dyed her hair hot pink, neon
green, black with streaks of grey and many other shades in-
between. The frequent variations in colour gave people the
impression that she did things without thinking or that she
was indecisive, but they were wrong. She was a brunette: if
you want pink hair, it takes commitment, patience, bleach
kits and latex gloves. When she began art school she grew
her hair out to its natural colour after a chunk broke off in
her hands, but her reputation for being flaky followed her.

"Nicole," he said finally. That's all. He hung up. Nikki
started dialling his number again, but stopped herself.

DAY 7: "SWALLOWING ANGRY WORDS IS BETTER THAN HAVING
TO EAT THEM."

Nikki's grandfather had been a sign painter in Poland
before immigrating to Canada and as an homage to him,
she bought huge sheets of glass wholesale and painted on
them. She'd found a book of church signs at a thrift store
and taught herself how to hand-letter a sign by painting out
slogans included in the book. They said things like, SIGN
BROKEN, MESSAGE INSIDE or HOW DO YOU WANT
TO SPEND ETERNITY? SMOKING OR NON-SMOKING?
She'd spend hours planning and then painting a single
word, making sure the slant of the A's were at the perfect
angle, that the O's were symmetric.

When Thomas and Nikki drove to the field for their
second photo shoot, she told him about her project.
Thomas said that the best church signs were in the States,
especially in the South. That afternoon they made plans to
take a roadtrip together. They could look for the craziest
church signs for her to paint and he could take pictures.
They high-fived, but Nikki wasn't sure if they were really
serious about it.

The next time they spoke, he called while she was working late at her studio. She'd been so absorbed in the act of
painting a Z that she forgot she'd hung another piece of
glass from the ceiling. When she bolted across the room to
answer her phone, she smashed headfirst into it. The sheet
shattered into pieces, cut her cheek and gave her a swollen lip. She pressed her hand to the top of her head and
discovered another cut on her scalp. The bright red blood
on her fingertips reminded her of how she'd dyed her hair
fire engine red for her high school prom.

Nikki had stitches the first time she and Thomas slept

together. She bowed her head and showed them to him and he touched the wound gingerly, felt the raised railroad of dark thread.

DAY 11: BOURBON AND ORANGE SODA.

Nikki turned twenty-two while they drove between Athens and Savannah. She had spotty cell phone coverage and kept missing calls from people who didn't know she was away or, if they knew, were fuzzy on the details.

Her brother called. "Are you okay?" he asked in his voice mail message. "What are you doing in the Smoky Mountains anyway?"

She hadn't spoken to him since the conversation at the campsite and by the time she heard from him, the mountains, their dampness and trees and green, seemed long ago. He must've been imagining her camping, fresh-faced and roughing it, while in reality she and Thomas had left that campsite quickly, annoyed by loud families staying near them. Instead of finding other places to camp, they kept sleeping in shoddy motels across Georgia. They thought they would camp more, but hadn't anticipated the sheer heat of a Southern summer and spent more time than expected sussing out cheap, air conditioned lodging.

Thomas and Nikki stepped out of the car to buy fruit from a roadside stand. The heat was so astounding that Nikki gasped. She ate an unwashed warm peach and threw the pit onto the road. They had a bottle of Maker's Mark, the seal unbroken, its red wax melted and smeared all over the top like congealed blood. Before getting back into the car Thomas poured some bourbon in a plastic cup and Nikki drank most of it quickly.

"Happy birthday to me," she sang.

Thomas took her face in his hands and squeezed her cheeks. She could smell the bourbon and peaches between them. They stared at each other and he kissed her nose. He hadn't shaved since they left and the scruff of his beard scraped against her skin.

DAY 12: OUTSIDE IN THE DARK I LOOKED DOWN AND SAW BLACK SPOTS. THEY STARTED MOVING. COCKROACHES.

On their roadtrip, Nikki wanted to keep records of what they did, but she couldn't bring herself to write full paragraphs in her journal, so she'd scrawl certain words: *catfish, rain on the windshields, wet socks.* Sometimes more than that. A description of the crabs on the beach at night, maybe, or how the Spanish moss that hung in lazy drapes from the trees in Savannah was used to stuff pillows.

She didn't write anything concrete about her days, no real narrative, and she definitely didn't write about the rest of her birthday, how they'd stayed in a motel in Tybee Beach outside of Savannah because they couldn't afford anything in town. They'd walked to the beach with the rest of the Maker's Mark. Thomas finished it off too quickly and told her that he'd slept with someone a few days before they'd left for their trip. Twice, actually.

"Why'd you do that?" Nikki asked. Her stomach hurt.

"I don't know," he said. He sat with his legs apart, his head hanging between them, heavy. She thought of a scene they'd witnessed on their first night in Nashville on Music Row: a woman, drunk and stumbling, crying, trailing after a man and saying, *you broke my heart, you broke my heart.* A country song.

"I wasn't going to tell you," Thomas said. "I'm sorry."

"It's fine." Nikki meant it and then a second later she didn't, but he'd already pounced on her forgiveness and wrapped his arms around her in a hug. He engulfed her. They rocked back and forth and then he threw up in a garbage can. Nikki stood by close as he clutched the sticky sides of the can and vomited a day's worth of bourbon and peaches.

DAY 13: HUSHPUPPIES ARE CALLED "HUSHPUPPIES" BECAUSE THEY WERE ORIGINALLY FED TO DOGS TO SHUT THEM UP.
On their trip Thomas didn't take many pictures and Nikki forgot to write down most of the church signs they passed. It was hard to think about art on vacation, and, truthfully, the signs she had in her thrift store book were better. The one sign she liked the most said, WHAT IF YOU DIDN'T BELIEVE IN ME AND THEN IT TURNED OUT I EXISTED. It wasn't clever or funny or a quotation from the Bible and it wasn't even grammatically correct. It was just a threat. It would be scarier, she thought, if she painted the opposite: if you did believe and then he didn't exist. It was better to not believe and be pleasantly surprised at the end.

DAY 15: OUTDOOR SHOWERS ONLY. YOU HAVE TO YANK A CHAIN AND KEEP IT PULLED TO GET THE WATER RUNNING. WE TOOK TURNS PULLING THE CHAIN WHILE THE OTHER RINSED OFF. LITTLE WHIRLPOOLS OF SAND AT OUR FEET.
They ended their trip on Ocracoke Island, a skinny, tiny island on the southern tip of the Outer Banks of North Carolina. They took a ferry from the mainland at six thirty in the morning. Nikki's favourite picture from the trip was one that she took of Thomas on that ferry. He's standing on the main deck wearing tattered army shorts and a black t-shirt. In the background you can see a little girl, blurry. You can't tell in the picture, but the girl spent most of the

ferry ride outside playing with the seagulls trailing the boat. She stood with her arms on her hips, put a cracker in her mouth and jutted out her chin, stubborn and brave. The birds swooped down and snatched the crackers straight out of her mouth. The gulls were fast, like military planes the way they dived down so quickly, and the girl, maybe nine years old, never flinched.

There were wild horses on Ocracoke Island. Nikki expected to be greeted by them running gloriously free, but the harbour was dotted only with little cottages and boats. It was quaint and pretty, but everything was too expensive. They managed to track down a campsite by the beach and there was a deep, sandy path that connected their tent to the ocean.

They never saw any wild horses. They drove to a lookout they read about in the guidebook and climbed three steps to a wooden platform for a better view. There were a few horses in the distance, small, stubby creatures, and they stood in a line, heads dipped into feed buckets. Their tails flicked the flies away, but otherwise they were motionless and lethargic in the mid-afternoon heat. *These days the horses are maintained by Ocracoke's agricultural society.* They'd skipped that line in the guidebook.

"Do you know Houyhnhnm?" Nikki asked Thomas.

"What the hell is that?"

"A language, from *Gulliver's Travels.*"

"I don't know any languages from *Gulliver's Travels*, Nik. I don't know French and I took it for eight years."

"Gulliver meets these horses and it turns out they speak to each other in a special language. He lives with them and learns it. In Houyhnhnm the horses don't have a word for 'lie.'"

"Why not?"

"They're so noble they don't even understand the concept of lying. They just never did it."

Thomas got uncomfortable. He thought she was leading him back to a conversation about the girl he'd slept with. They'd spoken about it one more time, the day after her birthday. They walked along the boardwalk at the beach and talked about it calmly, and they held hands and she told him again that it was okay. She meant it more than the night before. Afterwards they'd driven to Savannah where he doted on her, buying pecan candy, cold bottles of water, a big straw hat. She hadn't meant to bring it up again in Ocracoke, had just been reminded about Houyhnhnm while looking at the horses. People always talked about the part where Gulliver lives with the tiny people or the giants, but not the horses, and it was her favourite part.

DAY 16: THE AIR IS HEAVIER OUT HERE, SWAMPY. THE GRASS BY THE BEACH IS LONG, EACH STALK BROAD AND PALE GREEN.

When Thomas and Nikki returned to Toronto three weeks later, it wasn't as hot anymore. They had lunch together one more time before going to their separate apartments. When their drinks arrived, Nikki started crying. She kept dissolving into tears as they ate, but she insisted on staying. Thomas put down his fork and petted her hand. "Are you mad at me?" he asked. "What's wrong?"

Nikki wasn't angry and she wasn't sad, but she couldn't stop crying. Or, she was both of those things and more. Mostly she felt stripped of the protective cocoon of travelling. Far away from home nothing fazed her, but now that she was back she felt somehow betrayed by real life. By Thomas too for bringing her back to it.

It was like the confusion she'd felt after running into the sheet of glass in her studio. She remembered being utterly perplexed by how the air had suddenly solidified, how it had hardened and slapped her so hard she bled. A friend of hers who worked on the other side of the room said she'd exclaimed, "What the fuck," when it happened, but she didn't remember saying that or anything at all.

"I don't know," she said to Thomas. "I'm overtired."

DAY 18: THE RATTLE OF LARGE GROUPS OF CRABS SCURRYING ON SAND.

People asked, *what did you see on your trip, what did you do?* Nikki hesitated before answering. They didn't do much really: they drove and they talked and they looked at things. They went entire stretches without talking. This wasn't the answer people expected, so she'd describe the exact shade of red of a Red Velvet cake instead. Rusty brownish red, the bloom of a drop of blood in a cup of buttermilk. Nikki still has the journal she kept on the trip, but she never flips through it, although sometimes she's envious of the girl who wrote only little phrases, tiny summaries lit up by the glow of those heat-blurred days.

DAY 19: I JUST SAT IN THE GROIN OF A RIPTIDE.

Nikki's legs and arms were scarred up by mosquito bites for the rest of the summer. She got them at the very end of the trip on Ocracoke Island. They'd fallen asleep naked, and the mosquitoes had ignored Thomas and gone straight for her. They'd left the tent flap open a crack for air, and when she woke up in the middle of the night, her body hummed with itchiness, worse than when she had chicken pox as a child. The itchiness was more like a presence than a sensation; it hovered an inch above her skin, hot and throbbing. She wrapped herself in a sheet and when she woke up in the morning it clung to her, dotted with bright red spots of clotted blood. She'd thrown off the sheet and ran straight into the ocean, kicking up sand behind her. The water was freezing and frothy and angry. She sat down and listened to the foam fizz as the waves retreated.

At that point on the island the currents were powerful enough to be riptides. There was a sign with a diagram of the beach that charted out the anatomy of the surrounding ocean and Nikki copied it into her journal. According to the diagram Nikki was sitting in the groin of a riptide. It wasn't a bad thing. You're safe sitting in the groin because you're tucked in snug between the tides.

Thomas followed close behind and sat down. They sat for a long time while Nikki waited for her itchiness to subside. The sun climbed higher and coloured their shoulders and the apples of their cheeks.

Nikki also learned from the sign that if you're too weak to swim out of a riptide, you should just float on your back and allow the riptide to carry you away from shore until you're beyond the pull of the current. Fighting against it is what sucks you under. Once you're out in the distance, you can wave or yell for help, find a safe way back. She wrote that down too.

WHAT COUNTS

WHEN I MET NICK, I thought he was nice. A little dumb, but nice, and he didn't go to my high school, which was the most important thing. He came over while my parents were out and I played him "Country Feedback" on my guitar. As I fumbled between E minor and G, he leaned over and kissed me. The top of my mouth, underneath my nose. He missed. Nick's mouth tasted like toothpaste, and that night as I brushed my teeth, I got dizzy just thinking about it.

Nick was cute; he had these cheekbones. My aunt Lydia had a soft spot for paintings of Jesus, the airbrushed kind with photorealistic details. The strangest, my favourite, was of Jesus before the crucifixion. It's a close-up of his face. His eyes are rolled heavenwards and thin dribbles of blood are sluicing down his forehead, pooling in the gaunt hollows under his eyes and spilling over his cheekbones. Those cheekbones were as sharp as a supermodel's and when I was sixteen I was jealous of their definition, even if it was the blood drawn by a crown of thorns that emphasized them. Nick had cheekbones like the painting, like Jesus.

I kept falling for guys who looked like Jesus: long, wavy brown hair, too skinny. Hippies. After describing Nick to my best friend, Laura, she said, "Again with the Jesus guys, Esther?" I didn't know what she meant and when she pointed out the common thread between Nick and the last two guys I'd claimed to be in love with, I realized that I had a *type* and that type was Son of God.

My mother and Aunt Lydia immigrated to Canada from the Philippines when they were in their twenties. They left behind two other sisters, three brothers and their parents. They'd intended on returning, but then they both got married in Canada and stayed put, making up for their absences at family gatherings with gifts of money. I'd never met these relatives, but I knew their birthdays by the trips I'd take with my mother to a small store downtown that specialized in Filipino foods and had a counter in the back where she could wire money to her family, quickly and cheaply.

Lydia married another Filipino immigrant from her church, but my father was Irish, part of a family that had lived in Canada since the eighteen hundreds. They met at their first jobs: Mom was a secretary in the admissions department of the school Dad was teaching at. She was the first non-Anglo-Saxon to marry into his family.

After my mother and Lydia got married, their lives took divergent paths. The most obvious impact on me was that Lydia's children (three of them) went to Catholic school while I (an only child) went to an all girls', secular private school. My father was an atheist and my mother said she believed, but not enough to go to church and definitely not enough to get me baptized and confirmed. When I was a baby Lydia took this as a personal insult, some kind of forsaking of their shared childhood, but eventually the rift was mended. Whenever we visited, Lydia pushed bowls of pancit and adobo and lumpia my way, hoping that if she couldn't get through to me spiritually, she could at least physically stuff me with heritage.

I met Nick through my cousin, Mary. We were the same age, but by the time we entered high school had very little in common. We spent time together out of familial obligation and nostalgia for our childhood friendship, but judged each other in the passive-aggressive way only possible between relatives. She kept inviting me to her Catholic school parties because she was "concerned" that I wasn't meeting enough guys since I went to an all girls' school. While it was true that my life lacked daily male interaction, I managed to maintain a healthy stock of unattainable crushes. I usually turned Mary down, but one evening after a particularly passionate harangue, I surprised both of us and agreed to go to one of her stupid parties.

   I regretted my decision as soon as we arrived. Mary and her friends ignored me while I stood around and tried to look casual. I was relieved when I noticed Nick holding a beer and looking at a bookcase by himself. I walked over and saw that he'd pulled out *The Great Gatsby*. I'd written an essay for my English class on the use of eye imagery in the book, about how eyes were the windows to the soul and how Dr. T.J. Eckleburg's eyes on the billboard overlooking West and East Egg were like the paintings of Jesus Lydia displayed in her house: all knowing, wise, judgmental. I thought the essay was cheesy, but my teacher liked it so much that she read it aloud to the class. She didn't say who wrote it until the end, but later Laura said she knew it was me after the first paragraph, that she'd recognized my writing style. So, I told Nick, *The Great Gatsby* was special to me. "Cool," Nick said. He had soft brown eyes. "I'll read it."

After the party I told Mary that I liked Nick and she wrinkled her nose.

"His hair is gross," she said. "It's always greasy. I bet it smells."

"It doesn't, and he's cute." I countered.

"Esther," she said. "Sometimes you're so *white*." In the past few months Mary had taken to pointing this out, my whiteness, always witheringly, an accusation more than an observation. She said it when I talked about boys, when she flipped through my CD collection or when she analyzed my wardrobe. It made me wince and I never had a retaliation. *But I am white*, I said to her in my head, weakly. *Half, anyway*. According to Mary, Filipino tastes tended towards Filipino, Korean and black guys (no specific nationality provided). Italian too, and they didn't count as being "white." Her taxonomy of boys confused me. When I mentioned it to Laura she didn't understand either.

"Maybe it's because you're white," I pointed out.

She shook her head. "It's because I'm not racist. I don't believe in labels. I don't judge people by the colour of their skin."

"I don't think Mary's racist," I said, but I wasn't sure how to prove this. I suspected, however, that Mary's judgement of me had less to do with racism than Laura thought.

"Well, then she's just dumb."

I didn't have an answer for that either.

Mary said she'd talk to Nick and a few days later he called. I answered the phone and couldn't believe it when I heard his voice on the other end. The thrill of something unfamiliar. But wait, not a thing, a *boy*, a stranger, someone who lived on the other side of town, even. I knew my parents had plans on Saturday night and so, feeling bold, I invited him over.

I wanted to call Laura and tell her what happened, but she'd been acting strange recently. She would skip lunch without me or wouldn't return my phone calls. Even her sarcasm made me feel wounded more often than it made me laugh, so, wanting to preserve my enthusiasm, I kept the news to myself until I saw her at school the next day.

It was one of the first warm days of spring and we walked together outside, our sweaters tied around our waists.

"Can you believe he's coming over?" I asked. "We don't even know each other."

"Why wouldn't he?" she said. "He's a teenaged boy and you, a teenaged girl, have invited him to an empty house. He would be an idiot not to go."

I got the feeling that she was implying I was an idiot for being so excited about it, but I was still proud of myself, puffed-up from what I thought was an act of bravery.

Saturday arrived and I spent the day anxious and jumpy. I was starting to doubt that it had been a good idea to invite Nick over. I tried calling Laura for a pep talk, but her mother told me she wasn't home, so I called Mary instead and she answered right away.

"Why are you nervous?" she asked. "You don't have to sleep with him if you don't want to."

"That's not why I'm nervous," I said, wishing Laura had

been there.

"So you are going to sleep with him?"

I laughed at Mary's interest in my sex life, but now I had the additional worry that Nick was expecting it as well. As my parents prepared to go out for the evening, I went to their bedroom to see my mother. She was putting on makeup.

My mother was born breech and there's a Filipino superstition that says breech babies have the ability to be healers. Whenever my aunt had a bad headache or a cold, she called my mother. Mom always rolled her eyes, but she would still drive over to see what she could do to help. My father got a kick out of it too and at night I often found him sitting on the floor, my mother on the couch above him scratching his balding head while they watched television. "Maybe your mother can make my hair grow back," he'd say, his eyes half- closed like a dog. I was sceptical of these so-called powers, but sometimes when I had cramps, I would lie in bed and she would rub the small of my back. The warmth of her touch was maybe not healing, but it was soothing. Before Nick came over I craved that kind of comfort.

"Going to have a quiet night?" she asked.

I nodded. "What time will you be home?"

"Not late."

I worried that Nick would still be here when they returned. As I fretted, Mom walked past me in a cloud of perfume.

But when Nick arrived, I relaxed. We went to my bedroom and he was the one who noticed the guitar first. He asked me to play him a song.

Laura and I learned how to play guitar together the summer before. We met our teacher waiting at a radio station to get free tickets to a concert. He was behind us in line and overheard us talking about how we wanted to learn to play guitar and said he could teach us. We didn't think twice about accepting his invitation and every Thursday afternoon after that we gave excuses to our parents and met him for lessons. Sometimes they were at his place, a dark, skinny row house he shared with two gay men, but when the weather was nice we'd go to a nearby park. The three of us would sit cross-legged on the grass while Laura and I took turns playing his second guitar. At the time he was the most interesting person we'd ever met. We talked about inviting him to parties and laughed at how everyone would freak-out. As the summer wore on, his quirks became annoying. He was twenty-four, nine years older, and we weren't sure why he was spending time with us. We broke up with him at the next lesson telling him we'd learned everything we needed to know and wouldn't be coming back. He looked upset, embarrassed, but we ignored it and left. Together we're powerful like that.

When I played the guitar for Nick, it was the first time I'd played for someone outside of those guitar lessons. Nick was very attentive. He was quiet and leaned in to listen to me sing. And then we kissed, and I know I said it was sloppy, but it was also sweet.

Laura called me that night, late.

"How was it?" she asked.

"It was fun."

"That's great, Esther," she said, but I couldn't tell if she meant it. Either way, that night I fell asleep content. I thought about Nick and wondered if he was going to some-how factor into my life. I wondered if he would count.

At school Laura kept distancing herself from me. We'd known each other for years, but had only become best friends after bonding in an English class over our taste in music. I wasn't used to not talking to her multiple times a day. A school week passed, then a weekend, and we had barely spoken to each other.

One day my calculus class ended early and I made my way to the cafeteria to meet other friends for lunch. You could take a shortcut through the parking lot to get from one end of the school to the other, and I ran into Laura there.

"Hey," I said. "Where are you going?"

"Aren't you supposed to be in class?" she asked me.

"Aren't you?"

"They let us out early." She was holding a copy of *King Lear* and a green notebook we had bought together a few weeks ago. I had a purple one.

"Are you coming to lunch?"

She shook her head.

"Where are you going?"

"Nowhere," she said.

"Laura, what's going on?"

"Nothing, why?"

"Why aren't you telling me anything these days?"

"I don't have much to say." She left me standing there, baffled. I'd been angry about her behaviour all week, but at that moment I was confused. Sad. I thought of the time we'd walked away from our guitar teacher, how easy it'd been for us to turn our backs on someone we'd admired so fiercely at first. I didn't like that power used against me. I'd never been dumped, not by a boy or a friend, and when I sat down on the steps to steady myself, I was surprised when my eyes spilled over with tears. I cried just a bit, and then I went to lunch and hoped that no one would notice my shaky hands, my red eyes.

That afternoon I couldn't concentrate in class and so I wrote Laura a letter. It was six pages. I asked her if everything was alright and if she was mad at me and told her that she could talk to me about anything. *I miss you,* I wrote. I stuffed it into her locker at the end of the day and went home.

A few days later there was a reply from her in my locker. It was just as long as mine, on yellow, legal-sized paper. She was fine, she said. The letter was chatty and friendly and then, somewhere in the middle she wrote, *I had a dream and in the dream I kissed you.* I'd never had a dream like this about Laura, but I wasn't surprised when I saw it in her letter. I read it over a second time and tried to figure out how it made me feel. It didn't disgust me and it didn't scare me. It affected me and I didn't know what to do with that feeling. On a certain level, I understood, even if I didn't have an adequate response.

On Victoria Day weekend, Nick's parents went away and he invited me over. He picked me up from the subway station in his mother's car and on the drive to his house we stopped at a nearby convenience store and bought popsicles. Mine broke in the package, and I ate it with my fingers. His little brother watched television in the living room, but we ignored him and went straight to Nick's bedroom where he made me listen to Tom Waits. We were making out and then we had sex. I hadn't planned on sleeping with him, but it happened and it was nice and the only thing I regretted was that he kept Tom Waits playing on the stereo.

When the record ended, we heard small explosions outside. Kids were setting off firecrackers in the street for the holidays and we got dressed and joined them. Nick swiped a bundle of sparklers from his little brother, and we sat on the curb and lit them one by one, waved them around, the goldish yellow sparks flickering and spitting in the early summer night air.

After our first letters, Laura and I continued writing to each other, writing more than we actually spoke. We even stopped hanging out together at school and it was strange, but there was something satisfying about the letters, a feeling of connectedness that we hadn't had before. We wrote about everything, except I never said much about Nick and she never elaborated on her dream. The only time we stepped out of this pattern was shortly afterwards when she invited me to come with her to a show that weekend. It was at the house of a new friend of hers, she said, and she thought I'd like the music.

On the way over to the house Laura explained to me that her friends were Straight Edge, that they didn't drink or do drugs,

"So there won't be any beer," she said.

"That's okay," I said. "Are you Straight Edge now too?"

"Kind of," she shrugged. A boy in one of the bands was handing out wristbands he'd made with skulls and crossbones on them. We fastened them to each other's wrists. We sat under a tree and kept to ourselves as it got darker out, and then everyone went to the basement for the show.

The performers were hardcore/screamo bands, high school kids, and I didn't really like the music, but there was so much energy in the room. Everyone jumped and sweated and screamed along and I closed my eyes and listened to everything vibrate around me, wondered if the ceiling could cave in from such exuberance.

We left before it was over to catch the last subway home,

but right before we went inside the station, Laura grabbed my arm and we kissed, bathed in the light of the late-night TTC subway station. When you watch movies, television, whatever, it seems like teenage girls kiss each other all the time. It's so cliché. But at the time, it didn't feel like that. It felt essential and risky.

I got a scar on my wrist the next day, a tiny snip in my skin. I gave it to myself accidentally when I cut off the wristband. It wouldn't come off and I wanted to stick it in my diary as a reminder of everything, but the scissors slipped and there was a tiny gush of blood, and a band-aid, and then, a v-shaped scar. A few days later I pushed up my sleeve and showed it to Laura. We were standing outside school on our way to different classes. We hadn't spoken much since Saturday and hadn't sent any letters either, and we'd definitely not spoken about the kiss.

"Did it hurt?" she asked.

"Not really."

She held my wrist and studied the scar. Her hands were warm and I could feel her breath on my skin. "It looks like the bottom of a heart."

A week later my parents and I were at Lydia's for dinner. Before we ate, Mary said she wanted to show me something in her room.

She closed the door and put her hands on her hips. "I can't believe you're sleeping with Nick!"

"How do you know?"

"I just know."

"Does everyone?"

"I have my sources. You slut." She meant it as a compliment. "But Nick told you about his girlfriend, right?"

"Girlfriend?"

"They're not really together anymore, but from what I've heard, they'll be again soon. They're like, soulmates."

"Oh." I leaned against Mary's dresser, the wind knocked out of me. "I know about her," I lied.

"You're cool with it?"

"I'm kind of seeing someone else anyway."

"You're poly?"

I'd never heard the term, but nodded.

"Who are you seeing?"

"Someone from school."

"But you go to a girls' school."

I didn't know what I was getting myself into—polyamoury, girls—but I acted like I knew what I was talking about, that I had already pondered the philosophical and intellectual aspects of these concepts and was comfortable with them.

"Whatever." Mary shook her head.

"Don't say anything about it to anyone," I said. "Especially your mom." I imagined all of those paintings of Jesus directing their tortured glances at my immoral, pre-marital sex, homosexual experimentation ways. I felt damned.

"I will obviously not tell my mom. You're so white, Esther."

We both stopped talking, deflated.

"What do you mean by that?" My voice was smaller than I meant it to be. I was embarrassed to ask, but I wanted to know. I'd never thought seriously about the fact that I was Filipino or white until Mary pointed it out. "I am half-white."

"You're half-Filipino too."

"So what? Why does it matter?"

I wondered if Mary was on to something. I liked kissing Laura, but I didn't think about it the way I thought about kissing Nick. And I liked spending time with Nick, but I didn't like it the way I liked spending time with Laura. I was worried that I would only always be half of something. That I was wholly nothing. Or maybe Mary was implying that I was letting one half engulf the other. Was that even possible? And was it bad?

I expected Mary to laugh at me, but I could see that she was genuinely considering the question.

"I can't explain it," she said. "You can just do things I can't do." She meant it in terms of freedom, permission. For some reason she thought my whiteness was what justified my actions.

"It's a free country," I said to her. "You can do whatever you want."

"It's different," she said. "You wouldn't understand."

But I did understand. Kind of. She didn't believe she could make the choices I made, I guess, whatever she perceived those choices to be. The only problem was that I didn't know if I agreed with her. Our mothers came from the same background, were raised the same way and left their families at the same time, and yet had ended up leading completely different lives. I wasn't sure if it had anything to do with their heritage or race or non-whiteness.

Lydia called us and we reluctantly went downstairs. Everyone else was already eating. My aunt was convinced she had a fish bone lodged in her throat until my mother got out of her seat and touched her neck and then pretended to throttle it.

"It's a miracle!" Lydia exclaimed, swallowing for us vigorously. "I know you have powers. It's gone!"

"If only miracles were always that easy," my father said, scratching his baldhead. Normally Mary and I would join in the teasing, but that night we kept quiet.

Back at home I couldn't sleep. I tried writing a letter to Laura and then one to Nick, but I ripped both of them up and wrote one to Mary instead. When I read it over it sounded all wrong, more like my *Gatsby* essay than something sincere. I threw it out and wondered why it was so hard to say the things that should be said, the things that actually counted for something.

BABY TEETH

WHEN I EMERGED FROM THE FOREST I was six years old, all tangled hair and scabby legs. Skinny. Everything had been so blurry, a wash of murky colours and shadowy landscapes that when I saw the sun, my eyes teared up.

The old woman that found me was small, papery and greying, but she bent down and picked me up and carried me into her house. I looked up at her face and thought she looked like a cartoon. She had deep wrinkles and black eyes and when she opened her mouth a stream of question marks poured out.

I refused to sit at her kitchen table, so I sat underneath it. It seemed safer. And I didn't drink the water from the glass she gave me. I turned my head and saw her little grey dog lap at his bowl. When the woman left the room I scooted over to the bowl, held my mouth to it and drank deeply. The woman caught me in this position and in an instant the rumour started that I'd been raised by wolves, that she'd rescued this wild thing that couldn't speak or hold cutlery or sit upright.

The story was proven false as soon as she called the police, but the old woman was stubborn and told her version anyway, and too many people listened. I don't blame them. There are always people clamouring for a good story or for something otherworldly to believe in. I didn't speak for a week and it was as if I'd never had any human vocabulary. I've seen pictures of myself from that time and I have the wild-eyed and frightened look of a captured beast.

Here's another story: a mother leaves her two-year-old with a babysitter. Her six-year-old is supposed to stay with the babysitter too, but on the way over she'd started complaining. *I miss you, Mommy, I never see you. Let me go with you. Please?* The mother faltered. *Fine.* After the youngest has been dropped off, they stop at a grocery store and buy a bag of food. And then they drive for a long time. *We're going on a hike*, the girl is told. Before the two of them go into the forest the mother shows her daughter what's in the bag: juice boxes, a package of processed cheese slices, apples, animal crackers. The two of them set out into the forest. Sometimes the mother cries and the girl doesn't know what to do. Finally they stop walking. The mother tells her daughter to go back to the car. *Just follow the path, it's not far away. If you get hungry, eat.* She gives her the grocery bag and kisses her on the head. *Okay. Bye bye.* The little girl starts walking. It's like they're playing hide-and-go-seek. Her mother goes in the opposite direction.

After I was found and before I started talking again, sometimes at night in the hospital I'd whisper to myself or sing.

From my room I could see thin lines of light from the hall-way seeping under the door. I held my breath and strained to hear the reassuring hum of machines, the faint elevator pings. I would inhale and the antiseptic smell of the hospital burned my nostrils in a way I liked. It was different, sharper than the fetid, earthy smell of the forest. I knew my mother wasn't coming back.

The last guy I met at a bar had blue eyes, clear and pale and icy. He asked me to tell him something about myself. I told him that there are people in the world who believe I was raised by wolves.

"Are you really that wild?" he asked.

"Maybe," I said. "A little."

My sister and I lived with my aunt and uncle. They had wanted to stay in town, but when I started speaking again, when my mother's body was found, when the stories started spreading in newspapers, at water coolers, across kitchen tables, passing from person to person like a game of broken telephone, they realized there was too much to hide, so we moved to a different city, a different province. In the new city I was aware of how normal we appeared. We looked like a regular family: two lovely girls and a young, married couple. People assumed we belonged to my aunt and uncle and we didn't correct them. They changed our last names.

At school my class did a unit on the metric system and we stood in a long chain from shortest to tallest. I was right in the middle and our teacher gave me a red flag to hold up and wave. Since what had happened to me had happened to the most average person in the class, I worried that it could happen again. I would sometimes hear my aunt crying at night and it reminded me of the sounds my mother made when she cried, a soft crescendo of tears and gasps. I remembered my mother's cries more clearly than anything else about her.

I learned early on that things don't come out of nowhere. There is always a buildup. You just have to be attuned to it, like how sailors study the shapes of clouds to determine when they should set out to sea. I knew the significance of those dark circles under my aunt's eyes and I knew what it meant for her to be sad. So, as I got older I read books on survival. I wanted to be prepared for something bad, something sudden.

This is what you should keep in a survival kit: two boxes of waterproof matches, a Swiss Army knife, a good length of nylon rope, two garbage bags, a small mirror, some fishing line and hooks, dental floss (handy for repairs or fishing line if you run out), Band-Aids, a few flat packets of anti-bacterial lotion, instant soup, hard candy. And water, of course. All of this, minus the water, can be folded together and stuffed into a small bag or pouch. The average human being can get by without food for up to two weeks, so it's not a necessity. At age nine I kept my survival kit in my school bag. I didn't have a Swiss Army knife so I wrapped a small steak knife in a piece of gauze that could also be used in an emergency situation. I gave a kit to my sister and she ran around the house unravelling the dental floss. Our cat ate it and when the threads started hanging from his ass I got in trouble.

The day my mother brought me with her to the forest, she'd told the babysitter that she was bringing me to the mall for school clothes. When the stores closed and we still hadn't returned the babysitter got worried. There was no list of emergency contacts, no father mentioned. My mother had found the babysitter through an ad pinned to the corkboard at the grocery store. The babysitter called the police when it got dark.

I've never had a good sense of direction, but I know some tricks, like how to find Polaris using the Big Dipper as a guide or how, if you visualize a straight line grazing each tip of a crescent moon, the imaginary line that extends to the horizon is due south. These rules of thumb are useful, but when I was in the forest, I didn't know any of this. I was too young and everything seemed too dark. I felt as though I was a foreign object introduced to the land as a science experiment. I bobbed along and ate apples and cheese slices. I walked and then backtracked. Once I thought I saw my mother weaving through the trees, running, so I went in that direction. I sprinted and ended up at the edge of the forest, in a field near a house. I walked towards it, and saw the old woman weeding her garden.

That night at the bar, the blue-eyed man kept buying me gin and tonics and asking me questions. I told him about the old woman, how she looked for me and took photos and sent them to at tabloid magazine based out of Atlanta, Georgia. There were sensational, nonsense headlines like, *WOLF GIRL FOUND IN NORTHERN CANADA* or *RE-FORMED SHE-WOLF GOES TO SCHOOL.* I wrote a letter to the woman once when I was seventeen. *I wish I had never found you. I wish I had torn your fucking head off with my baby teeth.* She must have been dead by then because the letter was returned to me, unopened and unread.

"So what really happened?" the guy asked, "You got lost on a Girl Guide trip?"

"My mother hung herself from a tree and brought me along."

"Excuse me?"

"I was abandoned in the forest."

He put down his drink. "Shut up."

"It's true."

"So you saw your mother hang herself?"

"No, she left me before doing it."

"Why did she do it?"

"The usual reasons."

"Bullshit."

I've told this story to a few people, only late at night after they've had enough alcohol to numb the shock. Some of them believe me, some of them don't. I like the ones who don't believe me best and I always end up going home with them. But I never remember anything important about them, like their names or phone numbers, just some distinguishing features instead. Their eyes, maybe. Or their smell.

I've been reading about babies recently—how they grow, how they latch on to you, how they burst into the world, a squelchy mass of blood and tissue and soft, unfused bones. The bond between a mother and her baby starts so early, the baby growing in rhythm with her heartbeat, the same blood shooting through their shared veins.

I don't carry survival kits anymore, but I still firmly believe in Being Prepared, of steeling yourself for what will happen next. These days I find myself removing bags of milk from the fridge and cradling them to my breast. The cold plastic makes my nipples harden, the way I imagine they might when you're breast-feeding.

When I was younger I wished I'd been raised by wolves. I would burrow under my sheets and blankets, surround myself in pillows and imagine they were wolf pups, that I was one of them. I imagined being nudged to sleep by a warm, wet snout. I dreamt of animals with sharp teeth circling me and keeping others away.

Lately it's been the other way around: I'm the wolf. I see myself walking through city streets holding a naked baby by the scruff of its neck, in my mouth. The baby, a girl, squirms but then goes limp. She has blue eyes, like the guy I met at the bar.

With my free arms I carry shopping bags, my purse, a bottle. I hail a cab and climb in. I'm not sure where the cab is taking us, but I don't really care because what matters most is that I have my baby in my mouth, that she's with me, and I won't let her go.

SWIMMING LESSONS

MY FATHER DROWNED IN THE AEGEAN SEA, fifty nautical miles northeast of the port of the Piraeus. When it happened, my mother and I were at home in Toronto. It was early evening in Greece, afternoon for us, and I was at school when my mother found out. She didn't tell me right away. After class I went to swim practice and then I walked home and made myself a grilled cheese sandwich for dinner. I can hardly believe I didn't notice anything was wrong. That evening our phone kept ringing and I only saw my mother in passing, but I was always pleasantly weary after swim practice and associated the lingering smell of chlorine and shampoo with a kind of deep, sweet exhaustion, so I ignored the phone calls, didn't say goodnight and fell asleep early.

My mother, in those few hours after she found out there'd been an accident, hoped that a sailor in a passing ship would find my father and pull him on-board. At the very least she thought he could've been clinging to a piece of driftwood or a mermaid, anything, treading water and waiting to be rescued. Her hope finally waned, and at dawn she woke me up. She didn't bother getting me out of bed, and I was still lying on my side when she knelt down and rested her head on the mattress close to mine. I sat up, bleary-eyed, and looked around my room. Yellow-grey morning light filtering through the curtains, my mother on her knees at my bed, my bathing suit a damp lump on the floor from where I'd discarded it the night before.

Sometimes I wonder about those twenty-four hours, how it was possible that I could've lived through them without sensing some kind of overarching and fundamental change. Wasn't there a strong breeze or a sudden, quick rainstorm? Did I bite my tongue or feel my ears ring? I couldn't remember anything out of the ordinary. I mean I was thirteen when it happened. My father was in Greece taking care of some family business; it didn't occur to me to pay attention to cosmic signs to make sure he was okay. Afterwards I imagined that on the day he died, his ghost must've flown through our hallways, waved his hands in my face and tried to tell me that something was wrong. The electromagnetic forces in our house must have been off the charts, and I didn't even notice. When I got older I stopped believing in ghosts, but I still stubbornly berated myself for not figuring it out sooner on my own.

Hugo was the first person I told about this residual guilt, but it wasn't until years later. He said he'd felt the same way when his sister was killed and I felt a surge of love for him when he told me this, grateful that he understood, that he didn't tell me that my guilt was misplaced.

I met Hugo on a melty, early winter afternoon soon after I'd moved to Montreal to attend university. There had been a snowstorm in November, but most of the snow had melted, so I was sitting at a lone picnic table in Parc Lafontaine wearing fingerless gloves, trying to ignore the cold seeping through my jeans and into my bones. I had my journal open, but instead of writing I was doodling a picture of the man-made pond in the middle of the park. It had been drained, but the skating rink wasn't yet set up for the season, so it was just a big, gravelly basin.

Hugo looked over my shoulder. "Isn't it too cold to draw outside?"

My fingers were bright pink from the wind and my nose was running. "Not really," I said.

"Are you an artist or something?"

I shook my head. "I'm Zoe."

He walked away, but returned a few minutes later holding two small stones.

"You should use these to weigh down the corners of the pages." He handed them to me and they were round and heavy for their size, like overripe lemons, still warm from his hands.

On our first date I took the bus to his apartment and instead of going anywhere we sat in his living room and drank a bottle of wine. We got drunk quickly, and he turned sweet and started calling me a rotation of names. Baby, honey, darling, but with the G dropped and a Southern accent. *Darlin'*. I was Zoe only once and that was when we were in bed, his eyes first closed and later open. He said my name and then he came and we fell asleep tangled up, damp and sticky.

I woke up in the middle of the night, his lanky body sprawled out beside mine. Hugo was tall and skinny, six foot five, all bowed legs and noodly arms, more than a foot taller than me. His curly hair billowed around his head like a golden halo. He was snoring and I couldn't get back to sleep, so I went to the bathroom. I opened the medicine cabinet half expecting to find a stockpile of pills, but instead of drugs, I found hair products. Aerosol cans of hairspray. Pump bottles of two different kinds of gel. I opened a jar of moulding mud and smoothed its creamy contents onto my own hair. It smelled like flowers, like a manufactured spring breeze. I looked at myself in the mirror and my cheeks were flushed and my hair looked shiny, not in a greasy way, but in a styled, pretty way.

Hugo told me about his sister the next morning. Marie had been kicked in the head by a horse at a sugar shack when she was eight years old. She'd been on a school trip and the kids were fooling around while they waited for their hayride. Marie was tough, a tomboy, and she'd decided she wanted to ride a horse on her own when no one was looking. She approached one from behind, tried to swing herself up, but it got spooked and somehow kicked her in the forehead. She died from the impact.

Hugo, sixteen at the time, had been at school writing a history test. He hadn't studied and spent most of the class trying to peek at the answers of the girl beside him, but she noticed and blocked her paper. Instead of muddling through the remaining questions on his own he just sat there and looked out the window. He said it was snowing, so he watched the tumbling flakes and, right before the class ended, he was called to the principal's office. He thought he was getting in trouble for cheating.

When Hugo brought up Marie, he had no idea about my father. He told me about her because, he said, he'd gotten a good vibe from me the day he saw me at the park. Hugo was interested in energy and described people according to it the same way someone might point out a hair colour or height. He said my energy was warm and gentle and because of it he could confide in me easily.

I rarely spoke about my father, and one of the things I liked about leaving home for university was that no one knew anything about my background. My father drowned when a sudden storm blew over the small sailboat he'd only recently learned how to sail. He hadn't even told us that he was learning to sail while he was on what was supposed to be a month-long trip to Greece. It was the kind of story that was easy to spread, students sitting idly in the cafeteria, eating pizza and talking about the weirdest things closest to their real lives. My story was weird and real, and it was my defining characteristic. For years, people would see my picture in the yearbook and remember me only as *that* girl: the one with the father, the dead one.

As much as I hated to admit it, my father's death had gone on to shape my life in a permanent and irreversible way, altering my personality. It was an important part of me and laying beside Hugo, I was overcome with a desire for him to know my important parts, every single one of them. So I started by telling him about my dad.

"That's so horrible," Hugo said, his forehead resting on my arm, his hair tickling me.

The existence of these accidents in our lives, the sudden violence of them, bonded us. I skipped my classes and we spent the rest of the morning together, sometimes drifting off to sleep, sometimes awake and talking, and after that day I rarely slept in my own bed in residence at school.

I never believed in love at first sight, but I did believe

in love as a leaping flame, a freshly struck match. When it came I assumed it came suddenly. Or rather, I started believing this once I met Hugo. I was sure that what I felt for him wasn't infatuation or naivety or desperation. It was simply a beginning.

Hugo was a few years older than me and wasn't working. He painted, though. Sometimes he'd sell a painting, sometimes he'd work at a café or sometimes his parents would give him money, but he didn't spend a lot. He'd lived in the same apartment since he was eighteen and the rent had barely increased over the years, so it was still very cheap. It was a studio, long and skinny, the sleeping area on one end, the kitchen in the middle, and a living room at the front. When I'd come over, we'd hang out in the living room, the only room that got direct sunlight, and he'd show me the progress he'd made on a painting. I'd decided to get an English degree, but was having trouble concentrating on my classes. I was mostly interested in writing poems, so instead of studying, I would take out my notebook and write while Hugo painted, the two of us working in a steady, quiet rhythm. I loved these afternoons with Hugo. The hardwood floors gleamed in the sunlight and it was beautiful to sit there on a cold winter afternoon, the two of us talking about the meaning of his paintings or me shyly reading aloud my poetry, our socked feet pressing against the slick floors.

All of my poems were about love, which by default meant they were about Hugo. I was going through an e.e. cummings phase, so I wrote about bodies a lot and used too many parentheses. I always wanted Hugo to paint me, but he was painting trees that winter. Their energies, he said. His paintings were mainly abstract, rusty hues of paint scraped into swirls with stiff brushes or pallets, and they would dry into glossy, textured pieces that I would touch lightly afterwards to feel their bumpiness, exactly what you're not allowed to do in an art gallery. When I couldn't think of anything to write I'd look at his assembly of paints. I decided that if I were to paint him I'd use only yellows and oranges and reds. A fiery sunset, a flaming prairie.

Since starting school I hadn't made many friends and after I met Hugo, I didn't pursue the few I'd made. My roommate Susie was nice, and we'd gotten drunk together our first week at a bar with a bunch of other students from our residence drinking the worst watered-down beer. That evening I saw my undergraduate life clearly: going to class, trudging to the library during snowstorms, drinking the same watery beer with these new friends, staying up all night to write a paper or to exchange drunken sloppy opinions. I didn't mind my single bed, the shared bathrooms, the lack of privacy. I'd moved to Montreal craving something different and transformative, and at first I thought the experience of attending university would be enough, but then I met Hugo and realized that love was even better. His apartment was warm and easy to escape to. Whenever I went to my dorm to get clothes, Susie would be out. We started communicating through notes after I came by and found one folded on my pillow. *Are you still alive? I haven't seen you in days.*

My classes in my first semester were all introductory level and there were so many people in them that it was hard to strike up a conversation. I'd take a seat at the back of the lecture hall and be the first to slip out. Hugo's friends were mainly Francophone and because I didn't speak much French, I would often stay home to study when he saw them. I got used to us as a self-contained unit and couldn't visualize us in the company of others. I sometimes wondered what we looked like together. I'd catch glimpses of our reflections in his front window at night, and we were maybe ridiculous—he was so much taller than me, and his hair was always so messy, despite the hair products—but the strangeness was also what made us special.

I'd mentioned Hugo to my mother over Christmas when I'd gone home for the holidays, but she didn't know many details about him and I didn't have any pictures to show her, but I'd brought one of his paintings as a substitute. "It's interesting," she'd said, but I couldn't tell if she'd actually liked it.

It wasn't until a few weeks after Christmas that I got the chance to prove to someone that Hugo was a real person. My mother told me she was going to visit me in Montreal for the weekend, her first visit since driving me in the fall.

"I want you to meet my mother," I said to Hugo that night.

"Sure." He was sitting on the couch reading a magazine.

"She's visiting this weekend. I told her about you."

"Oh," he said.

Hugo wasn't close to his parents. My mother and I had naturally gravitated to each other after my father's death, but Hugo distanced himself from his parents, who, unable to cope with the sprawling mess of grief associated with Marie's death, became crazy in a way that pushed Hugo away from them. They'd decided that if they answered two fundamental questions, they would somehow get over their sadness. What concerned them most was whether or not Marie was safe and happy in the afterworld and what had they done to deserve her death. They shopped around for opinions. For their first question they found a medium who, with the help of one of Marie's unwashed t-shirts, fell into a trance as she attempted to make contact with her in the realm of the spirits. Hugo imitated the medium's voice for me—low and reedy and definitely otherwordly. Marie was fine, she told them.

For their second question, they settled on religion and concluded that the cost of their sins had been too great. Less than a year after Marie died, they sat Hugo down and confessed their sins to him. Affairs they'd had, money stolen from jobs. His father urged him to confess his sins too, but Hugo couldn't speak. He wracked his brain and couldn't remember anything he'd ever done wrong in his life. What did anyone do to deserve anything? Fat tears rolled down his parents' cheeks as they spilled their secrets and Hugo just sat there, silent. It occurred to him that his parents could do whatever they wanted and maybe they'd get goodness, but they could just as easily get fluky tragedy. It didn't matter. After he moved out, he hardly talked to his parents again and he told me that other people's parents made him feel uncomfortable too.

"I don't know, babe," he said. "Maybe it's too soon."

"What do you mean?"

"We just started seeing each other. Let's take it easy."

I'd assumed that this step was a natural part of the trajectory of our relationship. We'd been together for over a month, and although I knew it wasn't a long time, it felt more substantial than that. When I wasn't with Hugo, the yearning I felt for him was overwhelming, a rumble in my belly, something gnawing and impossible to brush away. I'd never felt that way about anyone else. Hugo looked up from the magazine and saw my disappointment.

"Fine," he said. "I'll meet her."

As much as I loved every bit of Hugo and told myself I didn't care what my mother thought of him, I cut his hair the day before she arrived, just a trim because it was frizzing out into clown wig territory. We were by the window and he kept his eyes closed as I cut the shaggier parts. My hair was a bit longer than his, and I would use his mousse to scrunch it up into curls. They came out more like frizzy waves, but there was something vaguely comforting about matching my boyfriend, or at least trying to.

"What if I don't want to meet her?" he asked.

"Why wouldn't you?"

"Adults make me uncomfortable."

"You're an adult," I said to him. "And it's really important to me."

"Is that a threat?"

When we were done, he swept the hair off the floor. Later I picked up a lock he'd missed. I recalled my high school geometry class, using a compass to draw perfect circles. His hair in my hand curled just like a Fibonacci spiral, the kind of perfection you find only in nature.

Maybe I shouldn't have been surprised that Hugo never ended up meeting my mother. Not only shouldn't I have been surprised, but I also should've known, guessed it from his original reaction, just as I should've known that the image I held of him had more in common with his paintings than real life. Unlike the first explosion of love, the unravelling was slow, a leak that I constantly scrambled to patch up.

My mother arrived, and I met her at her hotel. After we'd dropped off her bags, we went out into the city, walking to the restaurant I'd chosen for us. We settled in and ordered drinks, and twenty minutes later Hugo hadn't appeared. My mother suggested we order anyway, that he could order separately later, but by the time our food had arrived, I knew he wasn't going to come.

"Something must've happened," I told my mom. I used a pay phone out front and called, but he didn't answer.

I spent the rest of the day with my mother, and she only asked about Hugo one more time and then changed the subject. She asked me if I wanted to stay with her that night in the other bed in her hotel room, but I needed time alone. It was such a minor thing—a missed dinner date—but it was the first time I'd felt betrayed by Hugo. I hugged my mother goodnight and told her I'd come over in the morning.

I wasn't ready to go home yet and wasn't even sure what counted as home. I didn't want to go to the dorm and see Susie and most of my things were at Hugo's. My mother had given me one of her hotel keys so I had access to the entire building. I took the elevator to the basement, but there was nothing there, so I went to the top and found the pool and gym. The change room was humid and empty and there was a tall stack of folded towels by the door. I picked one up and quickly decided to go swimming. I hadn't been in months, and felt like doing something that would tire me out. I could go in my underwear; no one would know.

I jumped into the deep end, both arms straight in the air. When I was a kid, my father used to tell me that although he knew how to swim, something about moving from Greece to Canada made him forget. He said he couldn't imagine swimming in a pool or a lake and that even the ocean was different from the sea. When I was younger, I was terrified that I would jump into a pool and it would be the day I forgot how to swim too, but of course it never happened.

He was teasing me. When I bobbed back up to the surface I rubbed my eyes and flipped on my back. The pool had a domed white ceiling with a skylight on one end. It was getting dark outside and the skylight was a rectangle of grey among all the white. I floated.

Swimming is one of those things best learned when you're young. Foreign languages too. You pick up these skills without realizing you're doing anything special or complex. My parents insisted on swimming lessons, but I never learned Greek. My mother didn't speak it and my father only spoke it with his family who still lived in Greece. I'd hear him on the phone enough to get accustomed to the lilt of the language, but it wasn't until after he died that I decided I wanted to learn myself, as if it would bring me closer to him. I sat down with a book called *Learn Greek in Three Months*, but fell behind when it took me over a week to learn and memorize the alphabet. For hours I would sit and practice writing out the letters, learn the new symbols.

In Greek, there are two letters that make the O sound. There's omicron, which looks like the English O, and there's omega, which, in lowercase, looks like a little rounded W. Usually the omega will come at the end of the word, while the omicron will be the O buried in the middle, but this isn't a hard and fast rule. In my name, Zoe, the O in the middle is omega, not omicron. It's spelled zita, omega, ita. Ζωη. I remember being satisfied that my short name had two alphabet endings: the English zed and the Greek omega.

After my father died, I would sometimes find my mother crying. The first time I caught her was in the kitchen at breakfast, and I had no idea what to say, so I asked her what was wrong, even though I knew.

"Zoe," she said. "Do you know that your name means

life?" I shook my head. "Your father picked it. Your grand-mother was so mad when he didn't name you after her. He'd promised he was going to."

"I didn't know that," I said. But I did. My father loved this story, and would tell it to me often. Normally I'd cut him off, bored by my familiarity with the anecdote, but this time, my mother telling me the story and looking so sad, I pretended I didn't know, that it was the first time I'd ever heard it.

In the pool, I closed my eyes and wondered if I could fall asleep like this, in the water, on my back. I probably could. Maybe I could spend the night here, my mother asleep upstairs in her hotel room, Hugo in his apartment, Susie with the dorm room to herself for the hundredth night in a row. The water was warm. At that moment, it seemed inconceivable that anyone could die like this. Bodies float. You don't even have to try too hard; your body fat does it for you. I imagined my father floating in the sea on his back and looking up at the sky. Maybe in his last moments he didn't struggle or choke; maybe he was just carried away.

Eventually I got cold and annoyed in the pool, so I got out of the water and shimmied back into my clothes, wringing out my wet bra and underwear and stuffing them at the bottom of my bag. I took the bus to Hugo's, let myself in and hoped that he wouldn't be home either. But there he was, working on a painting, and he didn't apologize for not coming.

Hugo and I didn't break up until weeks later, but after the weekend my mother visited, things weren't the same. I was still staying at his place, but not as often, and sometimes he would outright ask me to leave. Finally, one afternoon as I sat on his couch watching him paint, he stopped, sat down next to me and told me that he thought it would be better for us if we didn't stay together.

"What?" I asked. When Marie was struck by the horse, she didn't die right away. She was still breathing when the ambulance arrived and kept breathing for a few hours more. The doctors couldn't control the swelling of her brain and one by one her organs started shutting down. When Hugo broke up with me, I thought first of little Marie lying in the hospital, her life slowly extinguishing. We'd talked so much about her and I wanted to keep talking about her.

"I'm sorry, Zoe," he said and gently patted the top of my head. "I think we need time apart. Things happened so quickly."

I understood what he was saying. I had become aware of it while I waited for him with my mother, but the problem was that I felt like I had too much love for him, that it had somehow exploded into a poofy atomic bomb mushroom cloud when I wasn't looking.

When I made it back to my dorm room, I was sheepish and heartbroken. Susie was there and I saw a fleeting look of irritation when she saw me slink in, but when I started crying she softened. I'd almost forgotten the way people treat you when something bad has happened. Tentatively. She took me out and we drank slightly better beer and for a few hours we played the role of girlfriends, laughing and close. She hugged me when I cried again when we walked home.

"What are you going to do now?" Susie asked softly from her bed after we'd returned, as if it wasn't an option to return permanently to our shared room anymore. She didn't mean it as if she were kicking me out, but she'd also gotten used to me being away so much.

"Maybe I'll go home for a few days," I said.

I had classes in the morning, but the thought of leaving was suddenly appealing, so I simply left. I left a note for Susie on her bed. I'd misread the bus schedule and arrived at the station three hours early. Hugo's was the only number I had memorized, so I called him while I waited. We hadn't spoken since I'd left his apartment, but I knew he would show up if I told him what I was doing, maybe not out of love, but out of curiosity. It wasn't like he had any other obligations, anyway. He came a half-hour later, his hair stuffed into a toque. Soft grey. I knit it for him for Christmas. It was lumpy and loose and when I held it in my hands I felt like I was holding the discarded skin of a baby elephant.

We sat next to each other and he put his hand on my knee and for the next three hours we drank coffee and talked. When it came time for me to board the bus, I swung on my backpack. It was heavy and threw me off balance.

"You can call me whenever," he said.

"Thanks," I said and turned and walked on to the bus. I didn't believe him. I took a window seat that didn't face in his direction, so even though I looked, I never saw him lope away. I thought about it, though, how his body curved over, the way he tucked in his chin and jammed his hands into his pockets. He walked like he was aerodynamic and as I thought about his walk, I wondered if anyone would ever study the way I walked the way I studied him.

I don't remember much about the last time Hugo and I had sex, just what happened afterwards. He fell asleep and I rolled on top of him. When he slept he'd curl into a ball, the smallest shape he could make, and I'd reach over and hold him. It was most effective if I just smothered him with my body, slipping my arms and legs into the floppy loops of his limbs, the way you're supposed to warm a person with hypothermia. Skin on skin. I loved the feeling of his breathing beneath me, a steady, comforting whoosh. That night I climbed on top of his sleeping body, and his hair got caught in my mouth and instead of disturbing our position, I just blew it away, working the hairs out slowly with my tongue. I wanted to say something embarrassing like, "You're the first person I've ever loved," but I didn't, and even if I had, I imagined the words would've gotten jumbled up in his curls or shot haphazardly into the black depths of the bedroom.

My relationship with Hugo lasted only three months, barely the length of a single winter. I felt kind of illuminated by the feeling of love even if it was over, like I was shrouded in a thin, lacy veil. It made me see things differently. Hugo's apartment was in a house that was over a hundred years old and when I first started staying there, I would lay awake at night and listen to the erratic banging in the pipes. The sounds made me think of poltergeists or restless spirits and at first I was afraid, but then, eventually, I relaxed. I didn't believe in that stuff anyway. I reminded myself of this as the bus pulled away, that I had nothing to be afraid of. This bloom of courage didn't come from Hugo, but at first, and for a while afterwards, I thought it did.

TIN CAN TELEPHONE

WHEN PEN MEDITATES, she doesn't immediately slip into a state of thoughtlessness. She needs to first transport her inner self elsewhere. She tells me that she always ends up in the same place: a beach, nighttime. She's never been to this beach, but she can imagine it clearly. She's standing barefoot in the cool, white sand and there are tall outlines of reeds swaying in the breeze. She's surrounded by salty, inky darkness. She peers up towards the sky and stares, and this is when the real meditation starts, I guess, as she pictures herself straining at the sky, the scattered universe.

We're sitting in yoga class and I steal her trick. I try conjuring her beach. But I get distracted. Do I imagine a beach by the ocean? Or a lake? I haven't spent much time near the ocean, but I imagine that its vastness must be powerful, more conducive to spiritual enlightenment. What does salty air feel like? Is it like a smoggy day in the city? Heavy like the air after a rainstorm? I open my eyes and look around the room. Pen's sitting in front of me and I can see the even, gentle heave of her breath. She's counting stars.

Pen's level of concentration reminds me of my older sister Audrey as a child reading curled up in the big chair in the living room. I would do everything I could to distract her, but she'd remain perfectly absorbed in her book. Sometimes I climbed up on her chair, pressed my knees against her thighs and stuck my face in hers. I stared at her freckles and counted them out loud. *Uno, dos, tres*. I'd picked up some Spanish from a television show and wanted to show off. Audrey would get annoyed and shove me away, but it wouldn't be until I counted to twenty or higher, some number that I didn't know in Spanish. Once, she pushed me so violently that I cracked my head against the coffee table and it took four stitches to close it up. When she was older she smeared cream on her face, a skin lightener, to remove the freckles. But they never went away, and in the summer multiplied into big blotches. Her freckles were the most gorgeous things and she hated them.

I started joining Penelope at yoga when I turned thirty. I thought I should exercise as I got older, but couldn't bring myself to go to the gym and had fooled myself into believing that yoga would be easier and kinder to my body. I was surprised when I left that first class with achy muscles, insecure about the inability of my body to fold itself over. When had I lost my flexibility?

The class always kicked off with a five-minute meditation session that made me more tense than relaxed. Five minutes doesn't sound like a long time, but once we were sitting there, the silence pressing against me, the minutes would stretch out slowly, like sticky, dripping honey. The part I liked most was shivasana at the end when the teacher would turn off the lights and we would lie on our mats in the dark. It was more like naptime than anything else.

Then I got pregnant and decided to keep attending class, hoping that yoga would foster a calm atmosphere for the baby. When I'm there I imagine that for an hour-and-a-half the fetus gets the chance to float in a serene salty bath, like I'm sending it off to the spa.

I haven't told Penelope I'm pregnant. I told our yoga teacher because I wanted to make sure it was safe for the baby, but I asked her not to mention it. "I won't say a word, Sara," she said to me. I could never remember our teacher's name and I couldn't believe she remembered mine. Then she smiled such a kind, trusting smile that it made me hate her a little.

Pen and her husband have been trying to have a baby for a long time. They wanted children when my husband and I were still preoccupied with student loans and starting careers and figuring out what to do with our lives. The thing about pregnancy is that you spend so much of your life trying to avoid it that it feels like a slap in the face when it doesn't happen right away. I assumed it would take me as long as Penelope, or at least three or four months, but after the first few weeks of seriously trying, I knew something in my body had changed.

I even waited a day before telling my husband, worried that he would be freaked out by how quickly it happened. *I* was freaked out. So I called Audrey. I hadn't spoken to her in months, but I thought someone removed from the situation would be the best person to tell first. A sister seemed like a good candidate. I dug up the last phone number I had for her, some small village in Ireland, but I couldn't figure out how to dial it. I had to look up the country code online. There was a weird international ringtone, like a long beep or Morse code, and then a monotone accented voice told me that the number was out of service.

During shivasana the yoga teacher walks between us and presses down lightly on our shoulders and touches our foreheads. Sometimes the touch makes me stiffen, but this class I like it. Her fingers are warm. I decide that tonight I'll tell Penelope about the baby. She'd be offended if I waited too long. Our teacher starts speaking again and then the lights go on and we head to the change room in a post-yoga daze. Penelope and I don't speak until we're outside. The cold slaps us, wakes us up. Spring hasn't quite settled in, but it's slowly edging out winter and the fresh air is a relief. "Do you want to get dinner?" I ask.

"Sure, why not? We have nothing to eat at home anyway."

We start walking towards our regular noodle house, our mats slung against our backs.

I knew Penelope's twin sister Kelly before I knew her. Kelly and I were assigned roommates in our first year of university. Penelope switched to our school halfway through second year and it turned out that we had more in common. When Kelly still lived here, the three of us often went out together. I learned that there's nothing more powerful than twin girls. Different hair and clothes, but those faces side by side can knock a person flat. And their voices in unison, like angels, something holy or strange. It's magic, I guess, how an egg can split in the womb and make two girls instead of one.

In my family Audrey managed to get the best genes. The

perfect combination of Mom's face and Dad's skinniness. The grey eyes, like my grandmother. Her red hair seemed to come out of nowhere, some great-great aunt no one remembers. I got the average genes, a slight chubbiness, brown hair, although sometimes in the sun you can see glints of that red. When my husband and I talked about having children, I imagined my genes mingling with his like they were at a cocktail party waiting to pair off. I silently rooted for the good ones, for that great-great aunt to make a repeat appearance.

It wasn't until I met Kelly and Penelope that I considered my relationship with Audrey. Even when living in different cities, the twins were close, and they talked or sent emails to each other all the time. Audrey and I, on the other hand, were friendly to each other, but we weren't friends. She was a few years older than me, but wasn't the type to dole out advice and I didn't ask for any either. By the time it occurred to me to regret this, Audrey had moved away. I started sending letters to her first, writing as if we were more familiar with each other than we had been before she left, and was happy when she wrote back to me in kind.

The last time I heard from her, she included a photo of her two-year-old daughter, Jo. It's a picture of the two of them on some lush green Irish hill, all red-haired and radiant. Jo was lucky to get Audrey's hair. I don't know much about Jo's father other than that he's an Irishman from her commune named Patrick. Maybe he has red hair too. At the commune they do things like spin their own wool and knit Fair Isle sweaters. They milk cows and churn their own butter and it sounds perfect, except for the fact that it can't be. Those kinds of things never work out the way they're supposed to.

That Audrey ended up in a commune in Ireland isn't entirely surprising. In high school she turned into a hippie. She grew her hair out long, almost the length of her back, wore bell-bottoms and these ugly purple-tinted glasses that I hated more than anything. Sometimes a friend would trace henna outlines on the insides of her hands. She didn't drink, but she smoked pot, and had a hippie boyfriend named Hayden. He had shiny long blonde hair and blue eyes and I was always too shy to say anything to him when he came over.

Audrey moved away when she was nineteen. She graduated from high school and didn't have any plans to go to university. She lived at home, idle, but then one day she picked up and left. Despite her pothead tendencies, she'd spent a few summers working at the Dairy Queen at the mall and those saved ice cream earnings funded a plane ticket to Europe. She was going to travel. She cut off all her hair and I didn't even get the chance to hug her goodbye because her flight to Paris took off while I was in school.

At first I assumed she'd return. She came back once for six months and another time for three, and then only when her passport required it. The last time she was here she told us about Patrick, but she didn't have a picture of him. The next time we heard from her, she was married (eloped on the commune) and we expected them to visit together. Thanksgiving passed, then Christmas and my birthday and her birthday, and still she was gone, no visit planned. My mother tried to convince her to come back, but it never worked. When I got married I hoped she would show up, but by then she was pregnant and said she couldn't risk the flight overseas.

I could've flown to Ireland to visit Audrey myself, but I wanted her to come back to us first. Anyway, she never invited me. Some families can deal with being far-flung. They book plane tickets to each other's homes, have long-distance plans. Pen and Kelly's family was like that, all of them situated at different points in North America, and they still managed to get sick of each other, to know everything going on in their lives. In our family no matter how much we missed each other, we weren't sure what to do about it.

But there were the letters. Not emails because, according to Audrey, the commune was too deep in the countryside. "Not even dial-up?" I'd asked, but she'd ignored the question. Instead of writing to us by the glow of a computer screen, Audrey would sit at her kitchen table with a candle and a stack of stationery. *It's strange, but this place feels like home to me,* she wrote once. *I know Mom misses me, but I can't stand the thought of living there anymore. I'm sorry.*

Maybe it wasn't Audrey herself that I missed, just the potential of our relationship, the idea that we could translate our letters to each other into something real and breathing. Still, when I read that letter I wrote back, *it's not just Mom who misses you.*

The last letter she sent me was right before my thirtieth birthday, a year ago. Unlike previous letters, it was unsettling. The picture of Jo was nice, but everything else was odd.

There were too many loose ends when I left, she wrote. *I was in denial back then. I was too young and every time I came back to visit I couldn't bring myself to do anything about it. I'm coming to terms with it now. Something about turning 35 (thank you for the birthday card) and getting closer to 40. My therapist has helped a lot. Do you remember Mr. Richards? He was married to our babysitter when we were still living at our first house. My therapist helped uncover some memories I had*

*blocked. Mr. Richards molested me when I was six. Maybe five.
I'm sure he didn't do anything to you. You were too little, just a
baby. You probably don't remember him. I blocked it out, but I
always knew deep down.*

There wasn't much more. For a few days I doubted what
she'd written. I didn't know that Audrey had been seeing
a therapist. Did communes usually have therapists? I also
didn't remember Mr. Richards or that babysitter. We'd
moved and the only babysitter I knew was a woman who'd
come to our house and sometimes bake cookies with us.

I asked Mom about Mr. Richards when I saw her next,
unsure of whether or not Audrey had mailed her a similar
letter. My mother talked about how much she'd appreciated Mrs. Richards for taking care of us when she went back
to work. "Mr. Richards? I didn't know him very well. He
was nice enough. How come?"

I didn't write Audrey back right away. I eventually believed her, but I felt guilty about my initial reaction and I
didn't know what to tell her. Her letter made me feel sick
and angry and sad, but mostly I felt futile. Imagine that
you've done something wrong and would like to atone for it.
Imagine that you don't know what you've done wrong, but
would like to apologize. That's how I felt. How could I say
anything? I put a response in the mail more than a month
later and only briefly acknowledged what she'd written me.
She didn't write back. Mom and Dad got a Christmas card
later addressed to all three of us, but there was no return ad-
dress. The postmark was different from the commune, out of
Dublin this time. No news about Patrick, but Jo sent her love.

You need to do things at crucial times. When I told Penelope that I was trying to get pregnant, she foisted fertility
literature on me, books that outlined how the menstrual

cycle worked. Everything depends on perfect conditions. Our genes don't mix like elegant rich people at a cocktail party I learned. They don't *linger* like that. Genes get slammed together, more like sweaty teenagers in a mosh pit, desperate for connection, foregoing tenderness for physical contact. It's easy to miss your chance.

I know that I should've written to Audrey right away. Called her. I choked. I don't blame her for not giving me her new contact information. I should've tried harder to track her down and tell her, *Oh god, I'm so sorry. Fuck Mr. Richards. Come back home.*

At the restaurant, I'm nervous and the squeeze of muscles in my shoulders makes me think of the baby even more.

"We're getting wine," Pen says. "I need it. Work today was awful, and yoga didn't help."

"I would drink," I say. "But I shouldn't."

"How come?" Pen studies the menu and doesn't see my expression.

"Well..." My voice drifts off and Pen puts down the menu. I tug at my hair.

"Oh my god, you're pregnant?"

I nod and feel tears coming on. They bubble up in Penelope's eyes as well and soon we're both crying at the table.

"I'm so happy for you," Penelope says and grabs my hand. I'm so relieved to hear her say this, happy that she didn't flinch. The waiter comes to take our orders and we laugh at how silly we look, mussed up from yoga class, streaky faced, but he doesn't seem surprised, like he sees this kind of thing all the time.

Later when we're slurping our noodle bowls and talking about maternity clothes, Pen's cell phone rings. It's Kelly, who lives in Vancouver now.

"What's up?" Pen twirls noodles around her chopsticks and listens to her sister. "I'm having dinner with Sara. I have lots to tell you. Big news." She gives me an excited kick under the table. "Not *my* good news. Listen, I'll call you later."

Often, not all the time, but enough that I've noticed the timing, soon after our yoga class Kelly will call Pen out of the blue. Unprovoked. Like, "I just thought of you; I wanted to say hello." I've already asked Penelope about whether or not they have a psychic connection, but I ask her again at the restaurant after she puts her phone away. She makes a face. She's been asked this millions of times in her life.

"Nope," she says, but then tells me something she hasn't mentioned before. "Sometimes it works like a tin can telephone. Usually it's just a pair of rusty cans and some frayed rope, but every so often I can hear Kelly on the other end. Or she can hear me. I don't know if it's a psychic connection or like, a kitchen sink science experiment that works by fluke. It's probably just coincidence."

"Probably," I say, but I'm not really sure. We finish eating and leave the restaurant.

"It's too early to tell if it's a girl or a boy, right?" Pen asks while we're walking.

"I have a feeling it might be a girl. It's just a hunch."

Pen hugs me and tells me again how happy she is for me.

"You'll get pregnant soon too," I say. "I know it."

She pokes me in the belly. "Don't feel guilty."

We separate and as I walk to my bus stop I think of her and Kelly. It must be the meditation that does it, that clears the air and prompts Kelly to call so regularly after class. I wonder if I can steal their trick to get Audrey to call me.

My bus arrives. I sit up straight in the seat and resolve

to think about Audrey while I'm meditating, not fleetingly, but purposefully. I will count Audrey's freckles while Pen stares at the stars on the beach. I start practicing right there on the bus, chanting Audrey's name in my head, concentrating on turning my thoughts into a radio wave and fortifying whatever weakened connection exists between my sister and me. *I'm sorry, I miss you, I'm sorry, I miss you, call me, call me, call me.* If I do it right, if I'm lucky, maybe the atoms in the air will align themselves correctly, pull themselves taut like a telephone wire so that my message will reach her clearly without interference.

BATS OR SWALLOWS

"MY TEETH," FRANCES SAID. "They fall out of my mouth when I speak." It was the beginning of summer and she was telling me about a dream she'd had the night before. "They're falling and I keep spitting them out like they're cherry pits, but no one says anything about it. You were there, and you ignored it, but I think you kicked a tooth away when it landed too close to your foot. You were barefoot. I was too, even though we were on Yonge Street? Somewhere downtown, anyway. I don't think anything's wrong until I take a deep breath, and it feels like I'm eating something minty, you know, really fresh? So I find a mirror and see my gums, empty. And then I panic and wake up."

Dreaming of tooth loss can be a symbol of death or sudden monetary windfall. Frances was worried.

"Maybe you'll win the lottery?" I suggested.

"No, I think someone's going to die. I've always thought I was psychic." Frances laughed when she said this, not taking herself seriously.

When I was in the sixth grade my friends and I wanted to know who was the most psychic in our class. This was before we knew anything about odds or statistics, so we made cards with symbols on them: squares, triangles, hearts, circles. One person would select a card and concentrate on the symbol while the rest of us would try to read their minds. We kept score of who guessed the most correctly, and in the end I was the most psychic, but that was mostly because I'd been responsible for cutting the cards and had cut them unevenly. After a few rounds I could tell what they were by their shape.

"Quick, what am I thinking?" I asked.

"You're wondering who's going to die."

"Sorry, lady," I told her. "Try again."

A few days later I left Frances a voice mail. *Hey, last night I had a dream too. I'm wearing a necklace made of teeth, human teeth, and some have roots. I show the necklace to people, you're one of them, as if they're a string of pearls.*

My boyfriend Nathan had just given me a pair of pearl earrings, these small creamy globes with dull gold backings. They'd belonged to his grandmother. The pearls reminded me of overripe berries, the way they look solid, but how even the gentlest squeeze will crush them, make the juice gush out. Nathan explained that a pearl is calcium carbonate fused together with a compound called conchiolin. Molluscs produce it as a response to irritating objects in their shells. When he wasn't looking, I bit into an earring, almost surprised by the resistance against my teeth.

My father called at 3:15 in the morning. I remember waking up and looking at the clock. "Janey?" He said my name twice. My little brother, Peter, had been in a car accident. I listened to my father, but also zoned out as I sat on my couch and looked at the outlines of frames hanging on my wall. I'd left a window open, so I hugged my bare legs. And then I put some clothes on, took my car keys and drove to the hospital.

Things I've made wishes on: dandelion fluff, white horses in fields, lost eyelashes, time (11:11, for example). As a teenager, I heard stories about the apparitions of the Virgin Mary in Lourdes, France. People would travel from all over the world to visit the site to be healed. I heard that if you prayed a certain prayer series to the Lady of Lourdes over nine days, something good would happen. When I recited the prayers in bed I felt a twinge of guilt for diluting the prayers of those more deserving of grace—the sick, the crippled, the elderly—but I kept at it anyway. On the tenth day, I went to school and got a good grade on a biology exam, and we got let out of last period early and I had a good hair day. It was completely banal, no miracles, but still fantastic.

When my brother had his accident, I was stubborn about my wishes and prayers. I thought—*if this is going to happen, it's going to happen.* It wasn't that I was angry, but that I felt useless. A wish was a puff of air; it was nothing. My mother wasn't religious, but she prayed and then she stopped because she said that whenever she resorted to prayer, something bad happened anyway. It didn't mean that God wasn't listening, it just meant that whenever one becomes that solemn it's because something serious has happened, something big and often irreversible. We stayed quiet, but that didn't change anything either.

Peter was coming home from a night out. He was driving our parents' car and it got a flat tire. He tried to change it himself, but the jack didn't work properly. He walked out into the street to flag down some help. There were only a few lights and he rushed into traffic too quickly. The driver he was trying to stop didn't expect him to be there. It happened very fast, the driver said, and it was so dark out.

I don't remember the last conversation Peter and I had. I think we talked about the summer, what we were up to. He'd just graduated from high school and was living at home before going to school in the fall. But I did get a postcard from him a few days after the accident. I couldn't believe it when I recognized his almost illegible handwriting in my mailbox, but then I realized that it was because he had addressed the postcard to the wrong apartment. It made its way to my mailbox weeks after he'd actually written it. It was from Vancouver, where he'd gone with some friends after graduating. He wrote, *How many vegans does it take to change a light bulb? Don't bother asking them, vegans can't change anything*, and then he described a hot dog he had eaten. Peter had gone through a political phase in his senior year and started eating vegan. I guess he'd changed his mind on his trip. It was a stupid joke. I didn't know what else to do with the postcard, so I tacked it up on my fridge.

Four days after the funeral I went camping. I wanted to go somewhere that felt and looked different, somewhere rural and dusty. When I told this to Nathan he said, "Definitely, let's do it. I'll find us a place to stay."

"I mean I want to go right now."

Nathan paused. "*Now* now?"

I nodded, and I meant it. He could tell I was serious and by the time we gathered our things and figured out a game plan, it was late in the afternoon. He drove us to Georgian Bay and we arrived after dark. I don't know how he found us a campsite on such short notice, but he did. He set up the tent in the dark as I sat at the picnic table and shone the flashlight in his direction. I wasn't very helpful, so he took the flashlight himself, and I kept sitting there, digging my fingernails into the damp wood.

In the morning we rented a small motorboat. It cost thirty dollars for the day, and before we left they gave us a map of the area, a photocopied piece of paper with little squiggly island shapes sprinkled throughout. I squinted at the map and directed the boat and tried to match up the landscape with the hand drawn scrawls. We wanted to swim, but not at the public beaches, so we settled on an empty-looking cottage perched on top of a small island made up of massive, flat slabs of granite. We anchored the boat and jumped into the water.

We had sex on the rocks outside the cottage. It reminded me of what Ted Hughes wrote about the first time he slept with Sylvia Plath: *you were slim and lithe and smooth as a fish.* It was like that. Nice. It was the bathing suit, I think, the swimming, the fresh air. And then I stretched out, stomach down with my cheek on the rock, which was warm from the heat of the day. I breathed and closed my eyes and thought about how things petrified, how when molluscs were upset they produced pearls, and how if I just lay here maybe things would harden into something good.

I didn't get up for a long time, and Nathan swam back to the boat to grab our towels. He held them above his head as he treaded back and then covered me with them. Later he forced me to get up, practically dragged me to the boat, and we chugged back to the campsite, me in the front, refusing to wear the life jacket, my t-shirt or shorts. We left before it got dark because I was feeling too far away from the world, even though that's what I'd wanted in the first place. Nathan took down the tent while I sat in the car, still wearing my bathing suit underneath my clothes.

The camping trip was an example of how after my brother died, I'd come up with plans, with ideas. Ways To Feel Better. They would make so much sense at the time, and then, suddenly, stop. Nathan humoured me, but even he sometimes gave up. I didn't recognize this pattern until long afterwards, even after it had been suggested to me by others, and so I would simply cling to my ideas, whatever they were, white-knuckled, and no one would be able to shake me of them.

One evening at the end of the summer I went over to Frances' house. She'd been away, taking some classes abroad, and I hadn't seen her since the time we'd talked about her dream about the teeth. Her roommates weren't home and we sat in the backyard. There were black birds flying high above us, shooting around in circles, squeaking. Their high-pitched squeals made me think they were bats, but Frances said, no, they were swallows. *Squeak, squeak.* Despite the squeak, definitely, swallows. Sailors used to think that swallows would pull them to safety if they were drowning and if that didn't work, they would carry their souls to heaven. They would get tattoos of swallows as talismans. The birds were darting around us, small and quick. You would need hundreds of them to swoop down and lift you up.

Frances had something like a talisman too, a tattoo on

the inside of her wrist. An initial, her own. It was small, and unless you knew it was there you might think it was just a birthmark or an errant splotch of ink. She didn't mean the tattoo in a narcissistic way. She meant it as a symbol that in the end, throughout your life, you always have yourself to rely on. I noticed it when she'd hugged me. I took her arm and looked at it closely. She hadn't mentioned it. She was sheepish. "I was kind of drunk when I got it. In Berlin. I could've chosen something much worse."

The ink was bluey purple and the letter was delicate. Peter had mentioned that he wanted a tattoo once, and had been planning to get one in the fall, was saving money for it.

"Are you okay?" she asked when I didn't say anything else after a few minutes.

I was having problems clearing my mind. I felt coated in a layer of wax paper. Crinkly, opaque. I felt like those scrambler rides at amusement parks, the ones that spin you into dozens of little circles, and just when you're getting used to the velocity of the swings, you're dropped.

"Here, let me show you something." Frances was taking yoga and she wanted to teach me what she'd learned.

"I'm not good at the breathing stuff," I said. "Or Sanskrit."

She made me get up anyway. We took off our shoes. She showed me how to bring the bottom of my right foot to the inner part of my left thigh, so that my right leg was jutting out to the side, like a flamingo. This was the tree pose. After you steady yourself on your leg, your root, you lift up your arms and branch out. And then you keep your balance. The trick to staying up is to focus on a single fixed spot. I stared straight ahead at the top of the tree across the yard, ignoring Frances's swaying profile beside me and the squeaks of the swallows above. I kept my arms stretched out and I curled my toes. I didn't stay up for very long.

"It's harder than it looks, isn't it?" she asked as I steadied myself and grunted. I just wanted to stand still. It seemed unfair that I couldn't do this simple move. When my foot touched the ground, I lifted it again, and then again.

For those few seconds I would think only of keeping my balance. When it worked, when I stayed up, I felt good. My rooted leg was strong and with my arms above my head my body looked streamlined, graceful. I got the idea that if I kept standing on one leg and looking up, if I kept focused and if I practiced this pose, maybe, eventually, I could train the rest of my body to stay focused enough to produce something beautiful, something permanent and solid.

WHAT YOU WANT
AND WHAT YOU NEED

BASIL IS WOKEN BY AN EARTHQUAKE. The floor shakes and the one painting he has on the wall rattles, but stays in place. He holds the sides of his bed and wonders what he should do. He closes his eyes and when he opens them again, the shaking has stopped. He gets up and stands with one foot in front of the other, arms out. Steady. And then he quickly pulls on his jeans and a shirt, grabs his coat and runs down the stairs. The ceiling of his bathroom started to leak on the weekend—how sturdy can this place be?

Outside he faces the building. It isn't swaying. He takes a cigarette from his jacket and smokes half. Each cigarette in the pack is marked off halfway down. He initially estimated halves as he smoked, but caught himself cheating. With the black marks he knows exactly when to stop. Basil decided to quit when he first moved into the apartment. He sat on the newly varnished parquet floors, shook the cigarettes out of the pack and measured and marked. He's still doing this two months later.

After two half cigarettes (the point is also to remind him of how much money he's wasting), he goes back to his apartment, this time taking the elevator to the sixth floor. The neighbour he stole Wi-Fi from locked the signal a week earlier (network name: GET OFF MY ASS) and because he doesn't have a television or a working radio, he feels alone, deprived of breaking news updates. He sits on his bed, takes out his cell phone and calls his wife, Hillary. He leaves her a voice mail.

"Hi Hillary, it's Basil. Did you feel the earthquake? I hope your new condo's okay. And that you're okay too, and Henry, if he's with you. I'm fine, in case you're wondering. Anyway, call me if you weren't crushed alive."

Basil presses the pound key and then six to delete the message. He leaves another one, but doesn't say anything about Henry. He deletes it a second time, this time leaving out the part about the earthquake. He's starting to doubt it happened. The final message is calm, casual and short, "Hi Hill, it's Basil. Gimme a call when you get this."

Basil and Hillary met at a New Year's Eve party almost five years ago. He noticed her because of her skirt. He saw it from across the room: short in the front and long in the back, sort of pleated. There was some denim in there and maybe plaid? It was ridiculous ("whimsical," a friend of his mused politely) and Basil was intrigued that she could pull it off and still look sophisticated. Sexy. He later discovered that Hillary often wore complicated items of clothing. She bought him a complicated shirt once. It had zippers all over and he was disappointed when he learned that none of them were functional.

Basil's parents named him after the man who owned the basement apartment they lived in when they were new-lyweds. He was an old Greek man, a painter, and he lived upstairs. He would invite Basil's parents over for drinks on his balcony or in the backyard, and in the winter he poured them cloudy glasses of ouzo to drink in his kitchen. When his mother got pregnant, she mentioned to him in passing that the only craving she had was for lemonade. For a week straight he delivered pitchers of cold lemonade to her in the morning until the craving passed.

The Greek painter killed himself when his mother was six months pregnant. Not at the house, but in the penthouse suite of a hotel downtown. Basil's parents were shocked when they found out. His children claimed the house and evicted them in the middle of the winter and so they packed up their things quickly and found a new place, this time in a real building where they wouldn't get the chance to de-velop a friendship with their landlord.

His parents never read the Greek painter's suicide note, but in it he left them a painting, one of his last works. It ar-rived at their new apartment a week before Basil was born. His parents knew they were having a boy and had already picked the name "Michael," but Basil's mother decided at the last minute that she wanted to name him after their old landlord instead. His father thought it was bad luck to name their son after a man who committed suicide, but his mother insisted and he gave in, worn out from the move and the stress of the birth of their first child.

When Basil was older he learned about Name Days. Greeks are typically named after saints and each saint has a day designated to them that's celebrated with even more fanfare than a birthday. Basil was the English translation of

"Vasilis" and his Name Day was January first.

At the New Year's Eve party, when Basil was introduced to Hillary she said, "Tomorrow's your Name Day!" and kissed him on the cheek. Basil wasn't used to people knowing that or being kissed by strangers. He looked at her funny, sophisticated skirt and her big smile and his love began to grow. They kissed again at midnight and then an hour later, and then for a sizeable chunk of his Name Day.

Hillary wasn't Greek, but her last boyfriend was, and she'd always liked the concept of Name Days, even though her own name didn't have an Orthodox saint cognate. They celebrated Basil's Name Day for the next few years. The last time was right before they separated and Hillary threw a plate against the wall. The act could've been mistaken for a Greek tradition, but they were just fighting.

Basil and Hillary were married within a year of knowing each other, both of them twenty-three years old. Neither had expected to marry so quickly or so young, but Basil proposed spontaneously and Hillary accepted, and before they changed their minds they followed through. They went to City Hall and she wore a grey-silver sheer dress and he wore the only suit he owned. Basil was secretly relieved that she didn't wear one of her complicated outfits. Their respective roommates and his parents were the only people who came. They deliberately kept the ceremony small because they thought it would be more meaningful that way.

Hillary's parents were in Europe, her mother was in Switzerland with a friend, her father on business in Germany. They came to Toronto two weeks after the wedding, stayed in a hotel and brought the newlyweds out to dinner one night and Basil's parents the next, before catching an early morning flight to Calgary to see Hillary's sister. For a wedding present, they gave them a cheque for fifteen thousand dollars. Basil was offended by the short visit and embarrassed by the large sum of money, but Hillary merely shrugged. He later found out that she hadn't told them about the wedding until the week before, precisely because she didn't want them to be there.

The first few months after the wedding were peaceful. They cooked together and watched movies and in the evenings Hillary would fall asleep in Basil's arms on the couch. They walked everywhere. The excitement of the first year of their relationship was replaced by moments of extreme, simple tenderness. Sometimes they would happen one after the other, quickly, incredibly, like multiple orgasms. Basil would lie in bed and think, *I am happy*.

There were little signs that things were going wrong. There are always little signs. The littlest: Hillary would get mad at him for not folding his clothes when he took them off or for leaving half-empty cans of beer around the apartment. She wouldn't just get lovingly annoyed, she would get angry. He got a sinking feeling about their relationship when they started saying mean things to each other without hesitation. "You're pushing my buttons," Hillary would say, shaking her head. And then she would lean over and push his, tentatively, like a tap on the shoulder, the way schoolboys fight, threatening, but never striking. They didn't hit each other, but they could feel the potential of it in their fists.

The biggest sign: when they decided to open their marriage and allow each other to sleep with other people. They were friends with a couple that had done this and were happily together. One night Hillary had drinks with the woman and when she came home, tipsy but not so drunk that she took back her words the next morning, said it would be the perfect arrangement for them.

Hillary had confessed earlier that she was getting crushes on men she knew and was becoming resentful that she couldn't act on them. The resentment, in turn, was poisoning their marriage. "It's just sex," she said. "I don't want a relationship with them, not like what I have with you." Basil agreed that maybe it could work. They read literature about open relationships together, found advice on the Internet, and worked out rules for themselves. It made them feel closer to each other, mutually flattered by the level of trust between them.

Basil created an online profile for himself on a dating website, but when he showed Hillary the messages a few girls had sent him, she thought using the Internet was cheating. "It would be too easy that way, you know?" she said. Basil didn't protest; he realized he wasn't actually interested in meeting anyone else anyway. Before he got the chance to discuss it with her, she'd already slept with Henry, and then everything fell apart.

Once Hillary said, *being mean to your lover can be a form of intimacy*. It was after a fight. "I'm glad we fight," she said, her cheeks rosy from yelling. "It means we're honest with each other." Initially Basil agreed. Real meanness is derived from familiarity and vulnerability, extracted from a moment of honesty. This was before they opened their marriage. They had been fighting about how she was feeling stifled. "You're too dependent on me," she sighed. In a healthy relationship, she said, you didn't need the other person; you wanted them. The difference was very distinct and very important to her.

"But you grew up rich, Hillary," Basil said. "You always

had what you needed, and if you wanted something, you could get it. What do you know about needing anything? You can't apply that theory to real people."

This was the kind of honest and mean thing that he would say to her. Her wealth was a sore spot, and she was embarrassed by its vastness, its depth, though she would never admit it.

"That's not what I mean. I mean I don't want to *depend* on you. I don't want to *need* you. Can't you understand the difference?"

"I don't see what's so wrong with needing someone," he said. "You have to be dependent on me, even a little."

Hillary didn't answer, which was her way of being honest and mean.

There was only so much honesty and meanness they could tolerate. Their lease was going to run out and they had to make a decision. Hillary said, "I want us to stay together," but she didn't look at Basil and he knew what she truly meant. Hillary, even in her most complicated of outfits, was easy to read. Basil stopped himself from saying this final mean thing to her.

Their goodbye was quiet. Maybe in the end all goodbyes are quiet. There was yelling and fights and tears at first, but at the end, after they'd packed up their belongings and found new places to live, there wasn't a sound left. Basil thought of *Don't Look Back*, which they'd watched together three times in one week the first year they were married. They rented it from a video store a few blocks away, but never returned it and when they split up, Basil was the one who kept it. There's a scene in the middle of the movie where Bob Dylan is sitting at his typewriter, mouthing to himself. Joan Baez is there too, singing and playing the guitar, so striking, but resigned. She stops playing, they tease each other and then she gets up, kisses him on the top of the head and exits the scene. And that's it. She leaves him. You can't tell in the movie because of the way it's edited, but that was goodbye—she didn't see him again for another ten years. Basil and Hillary watched the scene a few times to see if they could sense it, the weight of that departure, but they couldn't. Joan was quiet about it.

Basil is still in his apartment when his phone rings. It's Hillary. She got his message and was wondering if he wanted to help her paint her condo. Basil doesn't answer and she laughs at him.

"I'm just kidding. I feel guilty asking people to help me paint. I'm going to do it alone." Basil isn't sure if she's using reverse psychology, but insists that he's going to come by, that she should've asked him earlier. That's what friends are for and they wanted to stay friends, right? And, best of all, Henry wouldn't be there, although he doesn't tell her that.

The extent of their open relationship was Hillary sleeping with Henry. He was a friend of hers from university and had apparently been understanding of the rules of an open relationship. He never gave Hillary any ultimatums and he didn't ask her to leave Basil for him. This is what Hillary had told Basil, anyway. It was all her idea. After she slept with Henry, something clicked and she decided that she didn't want to just sleep with many men. She wanted to sleep with only Henry, and date him too. Maybe that was a bad sign for her marriage.

"Why do you want to go on dates?" Basil asked. "We're married."

"It's not like we act like we're married."

"How do married people act?"

"They don't sleep with other people."

"Sure they do. We've read books about it. They deal with it."

"Well, maybe I don't feel like being married to you anymore."

When the two of them separated, neither wanted to keep the apartment. Hillary bought a condo across the city by the lake and Basil stayed in their neighbourhood, in the Annex, near the University of Toronto where Hillary had been thinking of returning to start a new degree. To go to her new place he would have to take the subway to Union Station and then walk or take a long, slow streetcar ride. There was little chance of a random run-in at a grocery store or in the streets.

Basil was surprised that she chose to buy the condo. She had a view of the lake, which was nice, but that was it. She also had a view of the highway and who wanted that? But, Hillary didn't want to pay rent anymore. She didn't like any of the other places she'd seen. She could always sell it if she didn't like it. Her father was paying. All valid reasons.

Basil walks over, even if it will take a long time. He smokes a cigarette, more than half. A man standing outside the Scott Mission asks him for a smoke and he gives one to him, self-conscious about the mark, but the man doesn't notice. Basil stands with him and smokes his cigarette down to the filter, until it tastes bad.

"Did you feel the earthquake?" Basil asks. The man looks at him like he's crazy, shakes his head and walks away.

Hillary lives on the seventeenth floor and the elevator gets him there in less time than it takes to get to the sixth floor of his building. She's in her bedroom painting it pale blue. Basil picks up a brush and tells her about the earth-quake. She laughs at him.

"Things like that don't happen here," she says. "You were dreaming."

She tells him about the dream she had the other night. She got up, put on her slippers, and walked to the bathroom. When she switched on the bathroom light, the kitchen light went on. When she tried turning off the kitchen light, the living room light went on. It gave her a headache, so she crawled back into bed and pulled the covers over her eyes to block out the lights. And then she woke up. "I hate dreams that feel like real life."

They talk as they paint and the arm motions, the grandiose brush strokes, loosen them up. It's been so long since they've talked. After separating, they thought it was best if they didn't speak for a while. She broke the silence a week later and then they met for dinner once a week. They would eat and drink wine, but their conversations always felt halting and half-hearted. "Does Henry mind that you're seeing me?" Basil ventured once, carefully. "No," she said and kept drinking.

Basil asks about Henry again while he's painting and Hillary hesitates, but then starts talking. She's no longer dating him. She says, "I'm confused." She says she doesn't know what she wants.

"Oh? What do you mean?"

"I think a divorce is still a good idea."

"And you're sure about that?"

"I think so."

This makes Basil's eyes water. "Maybe we should give it another shot."

"Maybe we shouldn't have gotten married."

"I don't even know how to get divorced," he says.

"I'm sorry."

Mostly Basil does a good job of living, of going through his days assuming everything will work out for the best, but this afternoon, it all feels like too much. He excuses himself and goes to the bathroom.

He locks the door and sits on the bathtub hunched over, grabbing the edge. He wants Hillary back. He'd tried to block out this desire since they'd moved apart, but here it is, punching him in the face. He sits the way a person with a nosebleed is supposed to sit, his head above his heart. He tries to breathe. His shoulders feel tight. So do his calves and his stomach and the muscles running up and down his abdomen. He hadn't expected this, physical pain. A delayed reaction. A buildup of lactic acid. He doesn't want to lose Hillary, even after the mess of the past few months. Basil closes his eyes and tries to pinpoint the origin of this pain. The top of his stomach maybe? Behind his throat? He sits for a while, and then takes a Tylenol from the bottle sitting on the sink.

"Is the paint making you dizzy?" Hillary asks when he comes back. "I forgot to open a window." At first he thinks she says "pain," but realizes she means the chemicals. They look at each other. Before he can answer she says, "Maybe we shouldn't get divorced. I still love you. What do you think?" She's holding the roller in one hand and the pale blue paint is dripping onto a square of hardwood that hasn't been covered in newspaper.

"I don't know either, Hill."

"Okay," she says. "Do you want to have a paint fight?" It's the kind of thing she used to say when she wanted to cheer him up, but it stings when she says it and Basil doesn't understand how she can act like this, so flippant, while he feels wholly serious.

The two of them focus on the walls and Basil's pain slowly ebbs away. They chat as if nothing has happened, as if maybe they're still married or as if they never were.

The blue of her bedroom is the same shade as the sky in the Greek painter's painting. His parents had given them the painting when they got married. Hillary had been so moved by the gesture and she'd choked up when his mother told them. The painting was a standard landscape of a field bathed in sunlight. Too by the book to be something they would buy from a store and hang up, but the sentimental value made it transcendent. Basil used to study the painting in the same way he studied Joan Baez in the documentary. He could never find any signs of depression, nothing that would've indicated that its painter was about to kill himself. The landscape was cheerful, maybe uninspired, but bucolic.

"The painting would match your room," Basil says. It was their only painting and he knew she would know what he was referring to.

"Where is it now?" she asks.

"My room."

Hillary is putting tape around a light fixture. She stops. "Don't give me the painting, Basil."

When they're finished, Hillary says he can stay, but Basil goes back to his own apartment. He walks again, and by the time he gets home he's so weary, so goddamn tired. He takes off his clothes and closes his eyes, and listens to the water in his bathroom drip from the ceiling into the bathtub. The dripping is more persistent than it was the night before, like rain on a tin roof. He gets up, goes to the bathroom and checks it out.

The water is dripping in more than one place. He stands on the edge of the tub and presses up against the ceiling. The plaster yields against his touch. There are paint bubbles pregnant with dirty, dripping water and the ceiling feels alive, warm and moist, like skin. It reminds him of how Hillary used to sleep with her forehead pressed against his back. When she would get hot at night, he could feel little beads of sweat from her forehead against his skin. He goes back to bed and thinks about calling her, but knows that he shouldn't.

He takes deep breaths instead, what his mother used to tell him to do when he couldn't sleep. He breathes and hopes that he will sleep soundly and deeply, that the ceiling will not collapse in the middle of the night, that his dreams will feel like dreams and that he will not be woken by an earthquake.

ACKNOWLEDGEMENTS

Earlier versions of these stories have appeared in *Room Magazine, Kiss Machine* and *carte blanche.*

Many thanks to my editor, Sacha Jackson, and to Robbie MacGregor and everyone at Invisible Publishing.

For tireless support and exclamation marks thank you to Tony and Lita Vlassopoulos, Bonnie and Larry Emond, Kim Astley, Leesa Cross-Smith, Darcie Friesen Hossack, Samantha Garner, Christopher Manson, Emily Materick, Caroline Pelletier, Soraya Roberts, Susan Toy, Lesley Trites and Panagiotis Zervogiannis.

And thank you to Andrew Emond for everything, everything.

INVISIBLE PUBLISHING is committed to working with writers who might not ordinarily be published and distributed commercially. We work exclusively with emerging and under-published authors to produce entertaining, affordable books.

We believe that books are meant to be enjoyed by everyone and that sharing our stories is important. In an effort to ensure that books never become a luxury, we do all that we can to make our books more accessible.

We are collectively organized and our production processes are transparent. At Invisible, publishers and authors recognize a commitment to one another, and to the development of communities which can sustain and encourage storytellers.

If you'd like to know more please get in touch.
info@invisiblepublishing.com

Invisible Publishing
Halifax & Toronto

"Teri writes stories like nice days in the summer.
There's no rush, anyone you meet you're happy
to meet, you're up for going anywhere and doing
anything, you're okay being a stinking mess
because everyone else is, and you're so into the
whole of it being so completely right on that you
don't notice, until it's ending, just how scorched
you've been getting the whole time."

ANDREW HOOD
author of *Pardon Our Monsters*

The innocence and clarity of Teri Vlassopoulos's
narrative voice reveals new and unexpected layers.
The characters in these stories look for signs and
omens as they attempt to understand events in their
lives by framing them in abstract superstitions.
These stories are sharp, accurate, told with
balance and skill.

Teri Vlassopoulos lives and writes in
Montréal. Her work has appeared in *The
Art of Trespassing* (Invisible Publishing) and
*She's Shameless: Women write about growing
up, rocking out and fighting back* (Tightrope
Books). While she's been making zines for
ten years, *Bats or Swallows* is Teri's first book.

ISBN 978-1-926743-07-3

16.95 CAD

9 781926 743073

Invisible

www.invisiblepublishing.com